MW00617984

THE LAST GIFTS OF THE UNIVERSE

RILEY AUGUST

THE LAST GIFTS OF THE UNIVERSE

A Novel

HANOVER
SQUARE
PRESS

HANOVER
SQUARE
PRESS™

Recycling programs for this product may not exist in your area.

ISBN-13: 978-1-335-08179-7

The Last Gifts of the Universe

First published in 2024 by Del Rey. This edition published in 2024.

Copyright © 2024 by Riley Chirrick

All rights reserved. No part of this book may be used or reproduced in any manner whatsoever without written permission.

Without limiting the author's and publisher's exclusive rights, any unauthorized use of this publication to train generative artificial intelligence (AI) technologies is expressly prohibited.

This is a work of fiction. Names, characters, places and incidents are either the product of the author's imagination or are used fictitiously. Any resemblance to actual persons, living or dead, businesses, companies, events or locales is entirely coincidental.

TM and ® are trademarks of Harlequin Enterprises ULC.

Hanover Square Press
22 Adelaide St. West, 41st Floor
Toronto, Ontario M5H 4E3, Canada
HanoverSqPress.com

Printed in U.S.A.

For you.

1

You would think that while flying against a backdrop of foreign, dying stars, the last thing I'd have to worry about would be cat vomit. But lo, Pumpkin has violently expelled his hastily eaten breakfast. He sits there in the viewport of my cabin, grooming himself while I smack a cat-vomit-removal gel pad on the plush little rug next to my bed. The pad sucks in around the mess, locking in the scent before dissolving: vomit first, then gel pad. It leaves the room smelling like pine, a tree I've never seen in my life. I tap the rug with my foot to make sure it's dry.

"You little shit," I say, and Pumpkin pauses midlick, his pink tongue curled against his foot. He blinks at me, and then it's back to cleaning himself.

Pumpkin is smart enough to vomit in the toilet like the rest of us. He simply seems to go primal every now and then, as if to say: *But I'm an animal, remember?* Once, my brother, Kieran, put a prototype translator collar on Pumpkin. No less than ten colorful and vulgar demands from him for treats later, we decided it had been an unwise decision and removed it within the day. It's hard not to see every slight the cat has committed since as revenge.

Vomit dealt with, I plop back down at my desk, but it's futile. I'm distracted now, on top of antsy, and the recompilation I triggered just before Pumpkin's act of defiance has turned up nothing new. It's not the computer's fault. The first—and only—cache we've picked up in this cluster is simply bunk. It took half a day to decrypt and then turned out to be so irreversibly damaged that the data print amounted to Wingdings.

This is the reality of Archivist work. Most data caches we find—when we find them at all, and when they're undamaged enough to actually use—are mathematical proofs for theories our civilization has already discovered; strange numerical sets like financial trends; *Hello World* protocols introducing us to the species and culture of the civilization that left the cache behind; or, when we are extremely, profoundly, cosmically lucky, a new piece of technology, an answer, something groundbreaking that changes our worlds.

I would spacewalk without a cable for a find like that. I would leap from this ship into orbit in nothing but a shocksuit for the kind of find that led our civilization to the understanding of jump space, which is the only reason I'm even here, seven months and a couple million light-years of travel from our home systems.

Don't get me wrong; it's not for the fame. It's for my people and what could become of us if we don't find the answers we're looking for. But I don't think another scan of this broken cache is going to reveal any universe-changing secrets.

I slip on my favorite fleece vest (dark red and cozy) and some slippers (boring, wouldn't miss 'em if they voided). "Let's go see if Kieran's picked anything up," I say, and Pumpkin descends from his perch to follow.

My cabin door opens at a gentle touch, letting in distant, poppy music and a gust of hot air. Kieran likes it warm. Must be the other half of what makes us half siblings, because I prefer all cold, all the time. Pumpkin agrees with me, majestic orange fur drooping with the heat wave. Space is pretty icy, so we win out most of the time. Kieran can have the shared spaces and cockpit.

Pumpkin trails me through the short hall. We pass Kieran's room and the toilet, and then we're in what's officially called the comms on most spacefaring vessels our size. Unofficially, we call it *the den*—much homier.

It's the largest open area on the ship, a big dome-shaped center that leads to everything else: the cabins, the cockpit, the kitchen, storage, medical, and the suit-up area before the airlock and the exit.

There's a holoprojecting table surrounded by cozy benches in the center of the dome. It's where we could receive in-person (okay, holographic person) messages from the Archivists if they ever contacted low-level archeologists like us directly. Since we don't get those, and since I prefer to do archival work on my personal computer, we use the table for other purposes. Video games, mostly. And movies. These are not official uses.

On the walls, old-school strings of incandescent orange lights hang between planters full of cacti and small flowering shrubs from home. Most captains would call this an unacceptable fire hazard, but as it's just me, my brother, and our cat on this ship, no one can tell us to take it all down. What can I say? This is our happy place. We'll be spending most of the rest of our lives here, so we decorate. Even Pumpkin has a favorite part of the padded benches—his own personal seat, which he's clawed to absolute shit.

I follow the upbeat music to the cockpit, where the ambient lights are set to dim but the cycling of Kieran's rainbow dashboard shines it all up like a sun anyway. He gives me a lazy salute and takes his feet off my seat. "Morning, Scout!"

"Morning." I sit, and Pumpkin jumps in my brother's lap and gives him a good-morning head boop. Beats the hell out of vomit. "Find anything?"

"Weird blip earlier," Kieran says. Pumpkin's face has found its way to his cereal. "Just some debris in orbit, pretty sure."

I slump deeper into my chair. The *Waning Crescent*'s sensors can do a full sweep from orbit, scanning while a planet rotates through its whole day cycle, which for the planet below is three home-system standard days. It's nothing compared to the weeks and weeks we've spent getting from the last planet to this one, but I'm itchy to be off the ship.

The planet below, designated Planet 357 in the Beta Creon system of the Greerant Cluster (a mouthful, I know), is a slowly rotating, dead gray marble. Its jagged mountains are lifeless. Its oceans are dry. Its skeletal, sentient-made structures stand empty. There is nothing left.

It's always harrowing, seeing places like this, knowing that our work could be the difference between our own home worlds thriving or becoming...that. But those are the stakes. That's why we're here: to find out what happened to not only this civilization but every dead civilization we've ever found in the universe. Because as far as we know, ours is the last one left.

Seven hundred years ago, technology gave us the

keys to the cosmos, and we flew and teleported and phased out into the stars, arms spread, minds open, ready to meet the neighbors. What we found was a graveyard. Hundreds of once-civilized systems, all absent of life. Not destroyed, not nuked, or glassed, or buried beneath volcanic residue so completely that it would justify a whole world gone dark. Just...lifeless. Dead. And we don't know why.

The rainbow dash beeps—which is normal, nothing to write home about—but then it beeps *again*. Kieran starts, and Pumpkin retaliates by rolling off him and taking the cereal too. The bowl crashes to the floor, but Kieran and I ignore it and press together, practically cheek to cheek, to see the information compiling across the tiny screen. The *Waning Crescent*'s scanners have picked up a cache at last. They zero in on some kind of residual electromagnetic signature or something, I don't know. Kieran is the tech wizard, not me.

"Finally," I whisper. I can't help the relief. When you travel for home-standard months and months, you want to find something, anything. Something more valuable than a dead cache. Plus, it's going to be great getting boots on the ground.

"Looks like the target's in the middle of an old city zone," Kieran says, and begins collating the specifics into a data package: altitudes, air composition, crust stability, annihilation date. The usual.

Some of the structures on the gray, lifeless planet are so large that it's an easy thing to see them, even from orbit. I compare the orbital imagery with some of the terrain far below and think I find the right outcropping of dull white against the gray dust. A massive line of structures like mountains forms a broken circle around a crater that must have once been filled with water, or mercury, or some other liquid thing.

"It's in a lockbox, I think," Kieran continues. "Scanners picked it up easy because of the SOS."

"SOS?" I look at the readings on my own side of the dashboard.

That's unusual. Almost all dead, spacefaring civilizations we've discovered have stored various information in data caches, digital collections sealed in by long-lived electrical equipment our scanners are made to detect. Most caches are barely detectable and therefore stumbled upon, either dug up from ruins or captured from an endless trajectory through space, but the cache down there isn't just giving out its usual electromagnetic signal. Someone has amplified it, painted it with one of the most recognizable calls for help in the universe. This cache was meant to be found.

I remember the bargains I made with myself just minutes ago about jumping from orbit in a shocksuit or spacewalking without a cable if I were to find something big. I'm trying not to get my hopes up—SOS signals have given way to long-dead, unusable caches before—but I'm failing at it. It's been a long journey, and I'm ready to find *something.*

I compile a terrain-and-navigation data package and route it to our suit computers waiting for us near the airlock. Kieran closes the scan and powers down the *Crescent*'s thrusters so we lock into a stable orbital position.

"You ready?" he asks. He's beaming because he's probably ready to hit the ground too.

"Definitely," I say.

He leans back to look at Pumpkin, who's licked up all the milk from the bowl and is now considering one of the brightly colored *O*s. "Time to roll out, Pumpkin!"

"Meow," Pumpkin says, and lo, we roll out.

2

The dinghy lands nice and stable on the flattest piece of concrete Kieran can find within a klick of the cache. The rumble of the nuclear engine fades, and I'm left with that buzzing phantom feeling I've gotta shake out of my limbs as I stand. I give Kieran the thumbs-up. The hatch opens, lifting out and upward into the alien air of Planet 357. A chilly draft bursts in, and Pumpkin and I are revivified. Even under his little fishbowl space helmet, his majestic orange fur lifts with impressive volume. Could have been a model, but here he is. Little explorer.

I click the external audio for my own helmet. Some explorers of the cosmos use neural interfaces, which allow for what is essentially telepathy. But we're archeologists for a nonprofit organization, not the kleptocrats who run our worlds. We're poor, is what I'm trying to say.

"Give me just a minute for the thing."

"Again?" Kieran asks, but he takes one sad look at me and walks outside. Pumpkin follows dutifully after, little booties making footprints in the dust.

I have a bit of a new ritual I do planet-side when there's time for it, and so far there almost always is. There's no head archeologist to snap at me for holding up the procession across alien ground, no one to bark about breaking the law or, generally, futility.

I get futility. I really do.

I unzip my backpack carefully, but nothing floats out this time or threatens to fly away at a touch. Gravity is always weird in the graveyard. Sometimes there's none at all—almost zero—like the planet, at having lost all life upon it, gave up on its own too. Sometimes, it pulls me down so hard my knees buckle. Here, it's almost home-standard.

Extracting a palm-sized, bulky, dull red pouch, I zip my pack back up and follow after my brother, closing the hatch behind me.

It takes a little while to find an easily accessible patch of dirt. It's mostly urban where we've landed, all paved over and fortified except for the massive empty crater we're walking around. The almost perfectly circular path outlines the dried lake, with other, narrower walkways shooting away from the center like starbursts, toward other crumbled buildings, other crumbled city blocks. Standing like a decaying beacon against the gray sky to our north is a great shorn spire where our ultimate target is waiting. Its piercing upper half is cut off, collapsed to the side of the spire's base into a bed of smaller buildings destroyed by the fall. We got a good look at the carnage on the way in. Even partly destroyed, the once-spire stands ten times higher than any other building here that we've seen, drawing the eye.

We're halfway across the detritus-littered walkway when I spot it: a section of road so deteriorated that a dusty patch of earth shows underneath. "Found some," I announce.

Ahead of me by several paces, Kieran and Pumpkin stop. My brother leans over the railing to get a better look at the crater, and Pumpkin flops over onto his side to rest. I crouch beside the lifeless dirt and clear the patch of concrete chips with my hands.

Given that this planet once included an atmosphere similar to our own home's, I'm tempted to remove my gloves. This is difficult work with the dexterity-limiting puffiness of my suit, but obviously it's too risky to pull a stunt like that. Kieran would tackle me. The air is far from breathable, it's freezing, and some of the chemical compounds we picked up with the

Crescent's scanners could cause irritation or possibly a much more dangerous allergic reaction. Taking off my gloves would make this next part easier, but the consequences would be worse for me than the work. Plus, I don't want to get tackled.

So, gloves on, I go to task.

I uncinch the ties of my dull red bag and pluck out a generous pinch of the seeds inside. It's an amalgam of species, a mix of several desperate pouches I purchased back home when I learned Kieran and I had been given clearance from Archivist HQ to set out. Technically, our government has declared it illegal to intervene in the development of the local flora and fauna of any exoplanet, but this planet is dead. All the planets are dead. I wouldn't consider myself a lawbreaking individual, but I'm overlooking this one rule. Because this planet is dead, yes, but maybe it doesn't have to be forever.

We've terraformed planets back home. We've made gas giants into cosmic-filtration plants. We've invented the cure for the common cold—even if it is behind a ridiculous paywall. I'm millions of light-years away from home in a suit that lets me breathe on an alien world. All this, and you're telling me this world is dead forever?

I plant the seeds a little apart from one another and then fuss with the valves and hoses on my suit until

I can release some of the water inside onto the dirt. I give generously. This is the part Kieran has spoken up about. I can feel his eyes on me as I turn the dirt wet-black with my lifesaving stores.

"Scout," he said when he first saw me do this several weeks ago, on the planet before the one where we picked up that Wingding-filled cache. "I know you're still upset, but—"

"I've got more than enough left," I told him.

He sighed. "Just don't give too much." He hasn't pestered me about it since, but he watches me, every time.

Come back, I think, as I close up the external valve.

I stand beside the wishful garden. Normally, I'd activate my suit's hindsight module, get a glimpse of what this world was and what it maybe could be again, try to suss out some clue as to what could have caused destruction on this scale. But after the water thing, I can tell I'm trying my comrades' patience. It's time to move. A cache awaits.

Pumpkin boops my leg with his helmet, and I pat his back since I can't pat his head.

"Good to go?" Kieran asks.

"Yeah," I say and put away my bag of seeds.

It takes a lot of time to maneuver into the destroyed spire. Its entrances are caved in, its windows are shattered, its sewer systems are plugged. After a few hours of fruitless exploring and another hour of dedicated terrain study, I decide an up-and-in approach is the most viable. It's dangerous, but we've done it before. All planets are different, but most follow a pretty basic rule of gravity: wreckage falls down. This rule means that the higher up you go, the more likely you are to find an uncluttered entrance. That proves true this time, after a long, careful climb up the jagged, debris-covered side of the upper half of the fallen spire. We use it like a very steep bridge to reach the gap left by its shearing from the rest of the building.

We take lunch at the top, which—*hooray*—is calorie-loaded paste in a straw. It takes a few minutes to get Pumpkin to cooperate (this is always the tough part with him), but once the straw starts extruding paste onto his tongue, he laps it up gratefully. It's a few more minutes to make him drink water too, but again: grateful.

While we eat, we examine the hole. It's a long drop to the bottom. As it turns out, the spire held aesthetic rather than fortifying purposes. No floors were built into its long mast, and halfway up to where its length used to stand, we'll be descending eight, maybe ten, stories.

"Forty-five point seven two meters." Kieran's looking down the hole with a distance calibrator. Originally military grade and meant for snipers and long-range artillery, it was cast aside for better tech and finally made available for consumer hands. I only know this because he talked excitedly about it for two hours after he got it. It was a birthday present last year, from me. "We've got more than enough cord for it," he finishes, and puts the device back on his belt.

"You think anything up here's sturdy enough for the anchor?" I ask.

He hums and leans over our half spire, observing so closely that he's like a chicken pecking up bugs. Pumpkin waits at the edge of the hole, looking down like he's considering a heroic jump. I scoop him up right away. Big boy is as dexterous as an elephant on ice. He's going to have to go down anyway, so I attach him to the front of my suit early. The straps are meant for holding samples, tech, weapons, or the like, but they work just fine for Pumpkin, who lets his whole weight sag against my chest. It is an undignified position, but he's fought and lost this battle many times.

"These are solid steel," Kieran says, kicking one of the reinforcing bars revealed by the marble exterior's collapse. "And this is a nice piece of flat space for the magnetic lock. It'll do."

"It'll do," I repeat slowly, doubtfully.

"We'll be fine."

"Fine is *alive*, right?"

"Yes." He laughs. He goes behind me and digs the

climbing gear out of my pack. "We'll need to go down one at a time though, to be safe."

I hum, worried. I do not like heights. You would think I'd be immune to a fear of them, living in a spaceship and looking down at planets from on high all the time, but there is something very different about being seated on plush leather, enjoying a view, and being two steps from teetering over the edge. You float in space, okay? You fall on planets.

Kieran gets me hooked up and ready to go, and I stand at the edge of the jagged hole. I turn my and Pumpkin's headlights on in advance. It's dark down there.

"Ready?" Kieran asks.

I take a shaky breath and nod, lowering myself over the edge. Pumpkin does not like this either. His little feet flail helplessly as he lets out a protesting meow.

"Same," I say and let gravity take us.

3

Pumpkin and I land beside an old, utterly dry fountain and send the cord back up to Kieran with the motorized descender. The light coming in from above is faint, so I only get a good look at things when my headlamp is pointed at them. My circle of light runs over desks, dead-screened computers, chairs—maybe—with seats so small they cast doubt. Cracked and crumbled openings in varying stages of decay mark five equidistant points along the back wall. Above them, engraved into the ancient marble, is the shockingly universal sign for the atom. Not shocking because it's the symbol for the very observable thing, but shocking for how pronounced the symbol is, how utilized it is across all these dead civilizations, as well as our surviving one. Stumbling across it is like seeing home.

Aside from the debris and the markings, the only other thing of note is that it's eerily dark and cold, but that's nothing out of the ordinary in our line of work. So I let a very feisty Pumpkin out of his straps. He hits the ground like a shock trooper and bounds up the tiers of the fountain like he's chasing a mouse. He's moving so fast that maybe he *has* found something, but he hasn't. He gets to the top tier and meows.

"The real trick is getting down," I tell him as Kieran lands beside me.

"Whoa," Kieran says. "Little dark." He turns on his headlamp—an afterthought—and anchors the hanging cord to the floor so that it doesn't fly away, or whatever else an idle cord might do to inconvenience us.

"There's a couple paths going deeper," I say, and point them out with one hand while I pull the computerized tracker off my belt with the other.

"Will they get us to the cache?"

The tracker links back to the *Waning Crescent* in orbit, which is locked on to the cache we're here for. A grid map constantly scanning our new terrain projects the possible path each of the open tunnels could take to the cache, less than half a kilometer away, give or take. I study each theorized route with the tracker and my own eyes, then put the tool back on my belt.

"We're definitely in the right place," I say and lead

the way to the second opening I pointed out, directly opposite the spire's devastated front entrance.

We pass under the circular arch and into the ravaged hallways beyond. The halls have a similar circular shape. The maze of them reminds me of a network of veins. It's utterly different from our home worlds' architecture, not to mention the architecture of every other dead planet in the cosmos. We've become good at navigating alien spaces, though. It's part of the job.

Pumpkin alternates between trailing behind us and leading us, his tail shooting straight up like an antenna. Even though there's a big helmet on his head, his pink nose and whiskers twitch constantly as he sniffs along the ground. All our helmets come equipped with exceptional filters (courtesy of the Archivists' common decency), but maybe Pumpkin and his peculiar cat nose can pick up smells anyway. We turn one long, lazy bend, and I swear to all that is good in the universe there is a noise ahead. A clatter. I do not like clatters on dead planets.

I pause. Pumpkin pauses. We get along on our suspicious spirits alone. Kieran keeps at it a few paces before realizing we've stopped.

"Probably just settling," he says, like he's talking about a new house instead of a millennia-dead structure. "Scout, seriously?" He chuckles, a little brother making fun of his older sibling. "This happens all the time."

He's not wrong. Settling happens, sure. But other things can happen too. Like Remnants. I've read all about them and have therefore adopted a just-in-case mentality, which I believe to be quite prudent. Pumpkin's not well-read, but he seems to feel instinctually that something is off.

"Remnants?" Kieran asks, bored, a little impatient. Before I can even nod, he smiles and says, "They're so rare. We have thousands of Archivists out in the cosmos. How many have died due to Remnants?"

"Twelve last year," I say.

He relents a little because he can probably see I'm spooked. "Twelve out of what? A hundred thousand?"

I think a moment. "Roughly sixty-three thousand... four hundred and...fifteen?" I'm often equipped with useless trivia info. It's what makes me a half-decent archeologist, I'm told, nearly verbatim.

"Sixty-three thousand four hundred and *three* now, I guess," he jokes. I sigh. He sighs. "Scout, c'mon. If it was Remnants ahead, we'd already be shredded, right?"

That's not strictly true. Based on what I've read, Remnants are the only surviving entities of whatever likely obliterated life on all these dead planets, since they're the only things *on* these dead planets aside from ruins, and they don't exist anywhere else. They've only barely been dismissed as the actual cause of planetary annihilation because, *technically*, it's possible to escape them—enact a shield, shut a military-grade armory door, other such terrifying tales from some scant few survivors—whereas whatever happened to all these dead worlds was clearly inescapable. Instant.

Regardless of not being designated *the big cause*, encounters with Remnants are *deadly*. So deadly that there have only been about twenty aforementioned survivors in two thousand attacks. And that's just Archivist operator data. Black box recordings on archeologist equipment recovered from the sites of Remnant attacks are, frankly, harrowing, with their odd lack of sound, emptier than empty somehow, and the weird, distorted imaging. Survivors have talked about how cold Remnants are. Colder than tundra. Colder than *space*.

So, yes. Settling happens and Remnants are rare. But Remnants seem like an *awful* way to go, maybe one of the worst, and I'm not eager to sign up for the chance of being immortalized on the short list of victims. *Plus*—

Kieran is giving me a look like he thinks I'm overthinking things. He's tapping his foot, crossing his arms, all the impatient little-brother stuff. Tragically, he's right. We didn't come all this way *not* to get the cache, and idle time is wasted air. I try to take solace in the lack of signs. It's not too cold, certainly not for me and Pumpkin, and it's not unnaturally, ear-poppingly silent either. There's no frost on the steel of the stripped walls, no iridescent shine of something like, but not quite like, oil on water. Better yet, the first clatter was the last clatter. So I relent. I start walking.

Kieran smiles this big smile and gestures for me to go back to leading the way. Pumpkin meows and walks right against my ankles, trailing a few centimeters behind so he has the head start on any escape rush toward the exits.

We turn a few more bends, meet a few more dead ends, but eventually, after squeezing through a modest-sized fissure in the wall, we arrive at an enormous domed chamber. The walls are lined with computer screens. Some have fallen onto the dashboards below or the toppled, dusty chairs below them. Others remain on the wall but are cracked or completely crumbled, their inner electronics showing. The high ceiling and large amount of empty floor space make me think of all the boss rooms in the video games Kieran and I play, which makes me nervous. But there's Kieran, walking straight up to one of the video walls to get a better look. Pumpkin, too, leaves my ankles to sniff at a steel cup on its side. It catches in my headlight, surprisingly undusty compared to everything else in the room.

My belt buzzes, and I pull off the tracker to see it pinging the cache within a handful of meters. The *Crescent*'s readings are muddled by the distance and blockages, so the ping is vague, but looking around the dome, I'm certain I know where the cache is. I walk up to the circular raised central platform, some kind of command deck also lined in dashboards and ruined chairs. I can see a storage core through the railing ensnaring the deck, narrow and table-topped, with a barely visible piece of off-colored metal sticking out from its lid.

I climb up and through the gap in the railing. On closer inspection, the off-colored metal is absolutely the cache, with a glass-ball emitter on top and a broken or powered-down signal light welded to its side. It's stuck halfway out of the storage core with worrisome gouges in its sides, as though someone tried to forcibly remove it from the core's containment locks. But it's here. The cache is here and mostly intact.

"Found it!" I call.

Kieran bounds over right away, and I jiggle the cylindrical cache a bit to find that it's stuck solidly in place. Meant to shield valuable data, the storage core is hanging on with its remaining undamaged physical locking mechanisms. Removing the cache the rest of the way with force could risk damaging the information inside.

"Needs extraction," I say as Kieran arrives. He's already pulling off his pack, getting out his tools, and laying them neatly on the ground. He looks at the storage core, runs his hand over the dust caking its sides.

"Electronic and likely passcode locked, but if the mechanisms are mainly mechanical, I can have it out in a few minutes." He plucks a two-pronged tool off his mat and gets to work without waiting for an acknowledgment.

"Hey. Can we copy it first?"

For every cache where it's possible, Archivist methodology suggests downloading and copying any accessible files before moving the cache or even activating external apparatuses like emitters, physical object stores, or stored audio playbacks. That way, if you mess up extracting something, it's backed up. I wave my ship uplink at him, the device made for that very purpose.

He pauses his work to take it. "As soon as I find a safe way to interface with it, sure."

"Okay," I say, a little impatiently maybe. I want a guarantee the information will be copied, but he's the expert on extracting precarious caches safely. I give him the space to work, jumping the railing back to the dome's main level.

I make a long sweep with my headlight over the room. The ceiling is so high that even our combined ambient light doesn't penetrate its shadows, so I sweep there too. There's something reflective at the top of the dome that only shines when I tilt my head a certain way, but no Remnants.

I walk the room's perimeter, tracing the dashboards and screens built into the walls. My hand finds its way automatically to my belt, to the slight magnetic pull of the metal handle of my pistol. Early astronauts dropped so much expensive equipment that, a thousand years later, our suits have a low magnetic charge to help with grip that can be turned off internally for electronics fiddling. As for the pistol, I've never had much use for the thing. It ejects pinpoint force, so once I used it as a last resort to clear some debris. All Archivists are required to carry some kind of weapon for defense on planet-side missions. It's not like they'd really know if we didn't, but there's sound enough logic behind the mandate. Kieran has a sword.

I gasp a little as I accidentally kick another toppled cup. There are fewer than fifteen of them, but they're littered all over the floor: out in the open, next to chairs, under dashboards. Everything's dusty and quiet and…dead. It's easy to see it as a ruin, as a piece of alien history—not only for it literally being alien, but for how far removed from reality it seems. It is hard to grasp, but impossible not to, that these chairs once held people; these dashboards were once alight with bright buttons and data; these screens once showed other people or vids or numbers. This place was once alive.

There's a burst of static from the center platform and a flash of hazy blue light. Pumpkin hisses across the room, and my throat closes over a yelp. Light shoots up from the cache, and before I can see Kieran through the railing and screens and dashboards, the blue beam forms into a holographic figure.

"Kieran!" I call.

He stands up from behind the storage core, his face alarmed through the haze. "Sorry!"

"I am Organizer President and Interstel Councilmember Blyreena Ekstafor," the hologram says, the translator in my suit turning the wispy, breathy syllables into something I can understand.

At this I sigh with relief. My shoulders drop away from my ears. My jaw unclenches. This is a message cache, a recording, and Kieran's tripped a projector. I'm lucky that it's not a multiprojector, one of those balls of light that creates several holograms, usually all around the room. I would have had a heart attack.

"Give me a minute." Kieran ducks back behind the storage core.

"Did you start the copy?"

"That's what I was trying to do," he calls back.

Now that I know what's happening, the pitting fear has given way to a rising lightness in my chest: the excitement of seeing it, finally. Proof of life. A species I've never seen before or met, and never will. A walking, talking other being, even if they are a hologram.

The speaker continues on about the usual stuff we've seen a million times in message caches, either in training or in person on missions under experienced explorers. The speaker's station, their oath, information about the construction of the cache. It's no less fascinating the millionth time than the first.

The alien—Blyreena, I mark in my field notes—has pale purple skin that's slightly shiny, possibly due to an external mucous membrane or lots of oil. Their hands, four-fingered and slender, are held primly against their chest as they speak, their mouth a thin lipless line, their nostrils tiny slits. Their eyes are impossibly blue and iridescent, blinking with two sets of lids every few seconds.

They're coming to the end of the usual introductory spiel, and I'm growing worried about the integrity of the cache and how long it's taking for Kieran to turn the projector off. "How's it going over there?"

"It's being"—he makes a frustrated sound—"finicky."

I'm about to make a joke at his expense when Blyreena says, "We know now what it is that threatens all life in the universe."

My throat closes over whatever I was about to say.

"We know that what has destroyed the two ruined

class-A civilizations we've found has been the same thing, the same entity, and we know now that it has come for us."

I gape. My field notes, dictated by my verbal interaction, trail off with "..." in the silence. I manage to croak my brother's name.

"I'm trying, okay?" he calls.

"Don't," I say. "Hold on."

"This entity, which our scientific community has called *Endri*, is here in the Kyarmar system. It has already devastated Myr." I make a note: what we call the Beta Creon system, they called Kyarmar. I can't yet be sure that their body language matches my own species', but the way Blyreena hangs their head pulls something in my chest taut. "As Panev's Organizer President, I have authorized a worldwide evacuation effort of civilians and nonessential personnel to the Dremarius systems. Panev's most accomplished experts on the Endri, however, will be sent to Nebul in the Iari system, where our civilization's greatest minds are gathering to collate data points about this sincere extinction-level threat."

Kieran catches on at last, looking wide-eyed at the projection. "Holy shit," he whispers. Pumpkin is looking too, his tail flitting nervously.

"My people carry with them the last stand against

this final darkness," Blyreena says. "But my last stand will take place here."

"Is the cache copied?" I sputter.

Kieran blinks. "Shit. No. Not all the way, but it's almost—"

"Copy it!"

"I am!"

Pumpkin hisses. He doesn't like it when Kieran and I tiff. He's like an orange, fluffy therapist. But he isn't hissing at me. He's glaring at the ceiling, and I trace his gaze to an object that is falling from the shadowy depths near the center of the dome. Before I can make out what it is or warn my brother, it explodes in a rush of force, and Pumpkin and I are flying backward.

4

Remnants. *Remnants Remnants Remnants.*

I hit one of the dilapidated dashboards at the edge of the room and, on pure reaction alone, manage to scoop Pumpkin out of the air before he does the same. Thank whoever for those booties, because he's flailing around like a drowning person for air. My butt hits the floor after the dashboard cracks, and it's definitely something I'm going to feel later, but right now all of me is electrified with the energy to run, move, scream!

"Kieran!" I call, but the dust clears around the central platform, and that is definitely *not* Kieran.

A woman hangs from a cord, dropping fast from the shadowed ceiling like a puppet toward the cache. Sleek black uniform, state-of-the-art weaponry at her all obsidian-and-neon belt—and that stupid royal-purple *V* on the left side of the chest.

Verity Co.

"Hey!" I come to an embarrassingly shaky stand and settle into the dizziness. Pumpkin stands beside me in his ready-to-pounce position and hisses. Good boy.

The woman lands—steel-bottomed boots on steel platform—with a crisp *click*. She ducks beneath the storage core, disappearing into the whirr of extraction tools. I disengage my pistol and run forward, and yep, there's the back pain. But I push through, bounding up and over the platform's gut-high railing in a leap. I land right on top of Kieran and trip.

"Ow," he says plainly as my helmet bounces off the floor. It would take a lot more force than that to crack the thing, but my head rolls around inside like a bowling ball in a sealed trash can. All I can say is I've done my best, and I need a minute.

The grinding sound of extraction stops. There's a hiss of steam, and the Verity grunt rises above the storage unit with a beaming expression and the cylindrical data cache in a slender hand. "Thanks for disengaging the primary locking interfaces," she says, looking down at us. "We were having a tough time of it."

"I *told* you there was someone here," I mumble.

"Scout, really?" Kieran rolls me off of him, dejected. "United front, sib."

I look up at the high-pitched whine of a nanobeam pistol. The lady is pointing it right at my brother. One shot and *bam*—full of violent nanobots that'll eat him from the inside out. I'm mad as shit at him, but I do not want him to die.

"Whoa, whoa, whoa," he and I say, almost at the exact same time and pitch. He raises his arms. I sit up and do the same. "Please don't kill us," Kieran says, and the woman laughs.

"Don't give me a reason to," she says sweetly, but sweet like...sour candy that is way too sour. Or chocolate laced with poison. With one hand she fastens the big-as-her-head cache to the carrier strap on her chest. There's a pause, but her lips twitch slightly, and I bet she's communicating telepathically with whoever else from Verity Co. is around.

She's still silently mumbling when a rocket darts off the railing. Only, it's not a rocket. It's Pumpkin. He fires true and lands with his back feet on the woman's collar, then bats her helmet with his front ones, his suited tummy right in her face. Just: *bat bat bat bat bat*, like a pro boxer's flurry of hooks. Unfortunately, he's wearing those booties, so aside from the pleasing dull smack every time he lands a blow, it doesn't do much. She does scream, though.

In a quick, graceful motion that betrays her mercenary training, she puts the pistol to her belt and scoops

Pumpkin up by his armpits, hoisting him away. "Is this a fucking *cat*?"

"Um," Kieran says. Pumpkin's still swiping.

"Who the fuck brings a cat to space? I thought it was a dog!"

I should go for the cache. She's distracted, and it's right there, but I move a centimeter, halting at the back pain, and there's the zipping slide of another descender from above. A man slips down and lands beside the lady. Where she's slender and shapely and all that stuff the vids back home say a woman should be, he's bulky and broad-shouldered and strong-jawed, so… everything the vids back home say a man should be. He's wearing a matching matte-black uniform, Kevlar armor on the chest and shoulders, with that purple *V*, but *he's* packing what looks like a freaking mounted machine gun on his back. It's nearly bigger than he is. Verity Co. always comes packing, but this is ridiculous.

He pushes a button on the descender he's holding, and the cord falls from above, zipping into the device like a snake into a hole. "Told you it was a cat." His voice is like pure evil. A concrete grinder with demon horns. He probably laughs like the deathbots in those movies Kieran and I like. But he pokes Pumpkin's belly with a finger, and I swear, he smiles.

"Ridiculous." His partner shakes her head at Pumpkin. She sets him on the floor quite gently—to my grateful surprise—and he thanks her by going for her ankles. She ignores him. "Well, whatever. Ready?"

"Wait!" I blurt. "Please. Did you hear what the Organizer President—what Blyreena—was saying?"

"You mean the dead alien?"

"They said they knew what was destroying all the civilizations in the universe," I say quickly, because it's clear her attention is already spent. "They said they were going to enact a last stand."

The woman brings up a holographic display from a wristcomp and swipes through an indecipherable sequence. "Didn't really work out for them, did it?" she mumbles.

"Even so, do you know what that means? What that could mean?"

"Means a big paycheck," the guy says. Practically the Verity Co. mantra.

I bend my knee to stand, and his tree trunk of a gun autolocks on me. I can't decide if being eaten from the inside out or shredded from the outside in is worse. "Don't," he growls.

"Please," I say. I cannot believe this is happening, that they would overlook the implications behind what we've just found. The natives of this planet knew what was coming for them. They had a plan to stand against it, a plan that could become ours.

"Come on, guys," Kieran says.

Something beeps on the Verity grunts' suits. The holographic interface sucks back into the woman's wristcomp. "Ta," she says with a smile, and she and her partner and everything on them—including the cache—turn to light and phase away. Just, blink out of existence from here to somewhere else.

"Shit," I say. "We gotta go." I creak to a stand. "We can still catch them."

Kieran follows after me, Pumpkin at his heels. I'm building from a wavering walk into a jog. I need it to be a sprint, but I'm still dizzy from Verity Co.'s concussive grenade.

"They're gone," Kieran huffs. "Scout, they're gone."

"Teleportation can get them to orbit?"

"Well. No—"

"Then they're here. They must have gone back to a dinghy somewhere."

Pumpkin whines, and Kieran's silence is, as usual, his disagreement. I love them both, but after what we've found, we *have* to catch up with Verity Co. We just have to run back to our dinghy, break orbit, and restart our ship…all before they're able to jump to wherever they're going next. I know the odds are implausible. I know. But we have to try.

5

Despite all my frustration and adrenaline, I can't bring myself to move unsafely back to the dinghy. We follow all protocols getting out of the spire: ascending back through the severed tower, descending down the shorn half to the crater slowly, taking a break halfway across the walkways to drink water. It takes almost as many hours to get back as it did to arrive, and there's no sign of Verity Co. The dinghy hatch closing behind us feels like defeat, not victory. Kieran starts up flight protocols and autodocking procedures while I numbly buckle Pumpkin in. He's more compliant than usual, so he probably feels defeated too.

"Why?" I put my head in my hands. The dinghy is lifting off, making my anxiety-addled stomach flip. "Why here?"

"They're everywhere," Kieran says.

How I wish it weren't true, but lo. They really are everywhere. Verity Co. is the primary acquirer, collator, and distributor of alien information back in our home systems. See, they *copyright* all the information they collect, then charge a sum for the use of that information. Doesn't matter who uses it. Government. Scientists. Researchers. Grad students. Their own employees. They'd put the cure for death behind a paywall if they could, and they come close, trust me.

About four years ago, on my first tagalong mission for the Archivists, I contracted a weird virus exploring one of our home systems' moons. My fellow Archivists called it *popping the cosmic grape*, and it was one of those common, almost expected contractions rookies like me were prone to. Also it gave me blisters that looked like grapes. Anyway, I had to pay a doctor twice the usual copay because she had to pay Verity Co. for the patented information on how to treat me. Didn't matter that she'd seen enough of the case to treat it blind; she was using the info, so coin went in the slot.

Verity Co. stands in the way of everything the Archivists are trying to sow: freedom of information, respecting the source of that information, and using exoplanet data to empower the progression of technology and culture on our home planets.

I love our mission. I believe in it. And today, I've failed it.

"You heard what the person in the projection said, right?" I ask.

"Yeah," Kieran says. We're angled toward space, practically vertical. The whole dinghy shakes like it might fall apart, but we've done this enough times to know it won't.

"They knew," I say.

"You think so?"

"Why would they lie?"

"Maybe they just hoped," Kieran says.

The dinghy carries out its autodocking procedures once we're past the atmosphere and in orbit. It zeroes in on the *Waning Crescent*'s signal and pulls us into the claustrophobic underside bay. We disembark and run through the airlock, letting the med-tech sanitize and scan us for anything weird. It dings its approval, and we're finally back aboard, seven and a half home-standard hours later. We strip out of our suits and help Pumpkin do the same before rushing to the cockpit. The silence is aching as Kieran steers us through orbit and runs scanners, but there's nothing. Verity Co. is long gone.

"Shit," I say.

"We had no way of knowing they'd be there." Kieran closes the scanning data and gestures to the uplink I've been squeezing like a stress ball. He'd been able to get a partial copy from the cache, and here it lies. "Give me that."

I give him that, thoughtlessly, because instead I'm thinking about how I want to scream that I *knew* something was there, that the clatter had been our only hint. "Your radar didn't pick up heat signatures?" I demand, even though mine certainly didn't.

"It's Verity Co. You know they're stealthed so well they practically don't exist." He plugs in the uplink and pulls up a file called *PlanetDesignated357.Cache0001.copy.* He begins an upload to the *Crescent*'s mainframe.

"And you seriously couldn't detect their ship in orbit?"

"It's an automatic process. What more could I have done?"

"Look out the damn window, maybe?"

He turns on me, glaring, looking more hurt than mad. That pulls something taut in a line from my stomach to my throat. I know I've done wrong, but I'm too mad to stop. "I knew we should have been worried about that sound. *Settling.* What the hell *settles*, Kieran? The planet's dead."

"Okay." He turns back to the dashboard and starts opening files from the copy. "Well, while you're freaking out, I'm going to see if the cache has a civilization map we can use to find the planet they sent their science team to. What was it called?"

"Nebul," I say. "And I'm not freaking out."

"You're freaking out."

"They knew what was coming for them!" I cry.

Pumpkin jumps into Kieran's lap and circles a few times before curling into his namesake pumpkin shape.

"And we lost it!"

"I don't know what we can do about it now," Kieran mumbles.

"It's like you don't care."

"I care. But there's nothing we can do about it now. It's done."

I bite the inside of my cheek because what I have to say next isn't very nice. I don't want to feel this way. On some level I know he's right. There's no undoing what's happened. But I'm so mad at him. At myself. Because I could have done more. I should have done more. I could have tackled the Verity lady; I could have climbed to the ceiling somehow and made extra sure the dark was just dark and not a guise for something else; I could have taken the shot the woman had been aiming, because the data she was stealing was more important than my life.

More important than my life.

I wince in that involuntary, all-consuming way that

comes when a not entirely pleasant memory strikes like an electric shock.

We're only here once, I remember, and I'm in the hospital room with my mom, a long time ago. She laughs through a cough and pats my hand. *And what a thing my one shot has been.*

"I'm going to my cabin." I stand up, and pause at the arched entrance to the hallway. There's more I want to say, but it teeters between sympathetic and scathing. I don't trust myself to make the right call, so I leave quickly.

I lie and listen to music for so long that the peaceful acoustic beats actually manage to do something for my mood. Something, but not everything. Music's a miracle mood-lifter, but it can only do the job if you let it, and I hold on to stress and grudges like a lemur does to lychees. It's not my best trait, I know. I'm trying to let it go.

A notification pops up on my cabin's computer, a loud, specific *ding* that means it's work-related. I haven't received a call or message from Archivist HQ since receiving coordinates for the cluster we're in now, which means it's Kieran being official. Maybe he's a little mad too. I check the message.

Hey, it says, *I've found it.*

I lean closer to the screen, daring to hope.

Planet Nebul in what the native species called the Iari system. It's an easy day-and-a-half's jump away. Guessing I should launch?

I feel the day's worth of stress start to evaporate. My shoulders ease up from the buckling force of what I let slip from my grasp. President Blyreena sent their scientists to Nebul—*answers* to Nebul. Maybe we'll beat Verity Co. there. Maybe they'll be too stupid to decrypt and decipher the cache. Maybe they'll think they've found everything worth finding in this cluster and leave.

Launch, I send to Kieran, equally (and maybe a little spitefully) curt and official. In a second message I relent and write, *Thank you.* In a third: *I'm sorry*, but I can't bring myself to send it.

The ship rumbles in preparation for the jump. I don't know how all that stuff works. Quantum physics, teleportation, jump-space boundaries, yada yada. But I know the feel of the ship when it's preparing to leap, how space outside the viewports turns into long lines of passing stars and the black flurry of emptiness and dark-matter shadows. We jump.

Another notification pops up: *Almost half the cache was copied*, Kieran says. *It's all uploaded to the main server.*

Thanks, I write, and right on cue, another notification informs me data has been dumped into my Archivist drive. There's a new file, titled *Planet 357.* I stare at it a little while.

Relief at having a new course, a new chance at finding answers, has given way at last to guilt. It should have been me who found the star map in the cache copy. I should have been the one to find the path to Nebul. Kieran really backed me up today, and I need to do better. Starting now. I'm tired and mostly spent, but some things just have to be done right away.

I sift through the subdocuments until I find the map Kieran mentioned. It takes a little while, but I find the name of the planet we just left. Not the number-ridden designation the cosmic maps from back home gave it, but the name Blyreena and their people knew it as.

I change the file name to *Panev.*

6

I scour the cache copy for any reference to the world-ending entity Blyreena mentioned: *Endri.* The only thing that comes up is a data collation corrupted by the incomplete copy. Information on what destroyed Panev—on what possibly destroyed every dead civilization we've ever come across—was right there. *Right there.* And Verity Co. made off with it. Before I can get lost in the frustration again, I take a deep breath and move on to the files my assistive AI program has tagged as *Hello World*.

Hello World protocol is surprisingly, cosmically common, included in almost every alien cache we find. Packages include biological data about the dominant native species, cultural overviews, brief notes on systems of government, moral philosophies, and usually a verbose, well-meaning message of greeting to whoever might find the data. We Archivists find these packages everywhere, in everything from message caches like the one we just lost, to endlessly moving satellite beacons still on a trajectory from where they were launched. It's like every species in the universe was excited to meet someone—to share a little of themselves and their culture—but no one got the chance.

According to the data, Panev was the capital world in the capital system of the Stelhari, the planet's native intelligent species the person in the hologram belonged to. Stelhari were the only intelligent species to arise from their planet and the only intelligent species across their eight colonized systems.

I compare the detailed biological references of their bodies to my memory of the hologram: the four-fingered hands, the flat faces, the iridescent eyes. Where Blyreena had been slightly purplish, skin tones varied from cool blues and greens to dusty reds and stark crimson. Male Stelhari were multicolored, with splashes of hues like a painter's palette across their skin. Like many species, the Stelhari documented only a male and a female sex, though four common sets of pronouns existed for four distinct gender and social identities. I cross-reference these with the names provided in the docket of cache-contributors to find all four represented, and discover that Blyreena used female-associated pronouns. I flag this in the translator.

Her authored files, beginning with the greeting Kieran triggered planet-side, are complete. In her language, they're labeled as *Last Stand*. Seeing it causes the same stomach-flipping sensation as hearing it did. I'm hoping she's left me something here about what that last stand was. Instructions. Preparations. Considerations. How does a civilization defend against something so evidently destructive, and where did she and her people go wrong? Why did Panev still fall?

I click open the file. My cabin lights dim, and Blyreena's hologram appears before me and speaks.

Recording Playback 1.0023.498.x

Speaker and Authorizer: Organizer President, Interstel Councilmember Sy. Blyreena Ekstafor

Rotation 2, Mayak Harvest, 3550

This is my last stand. This is what I can do in the face of the entity coming to this world. In choosing where to begin, it is tempting to start from the here and now and work backward, or start at the very beginning, when I was but very small and living here in the capital hub of our world, in the very shadow of the Sciences Spire I now record this in. In those days when I would stare out at the lake with my father, when the smell of his cooking would fill the house exactly an hour before Dad came home, whereupon we would join on the sofa and watch our shows. Mystery was Father's favorite, but Dad and I, we liked cartoons best. Or maybe he just liked them for me.

But I can't—I can't—because my time is limited. Because I could spend more years recounting my fond memories of my family than I spent actually living them, and because in these last moments, or days, or weeks that I have left, watching my people leave for another world, I want to document something more recent and (forgive me, Dad, Father) something more special. Something that changed everything.

I want to talk about Ovlan and the last gift he gave to me.

I pause the recording.

It's not what I was expecting. It's not what we usually find in caches like this. Blyreena is calm and stoic, with an earnestness that can't possibly be a mistake of translation for how real and moving it is. But she's talking about her life, not the entity. Not the doom. Not the Endri. Not—in sad, simple terms—what I'm here for.

And yet this is the only tangible thing I have of that cache we lost. The only thing aside from coldly delivered scientific facts about the Stelhari.

Maybe there's something more here. Maybe I can dive back into the recording, root out the use in the mundanity of Blyreena's story, find snippets of evidence that account for it being her last stand against the Endri. But I'm fried. I'm fried, disappointed, and still mad as hell at Verity Co. I can't believe they're here. There are a million systems in the universe, and damn it all, they're *here*, and they've stolen the closest thing I've ever seen to a firsthand experience with the entity slaughtering all these worlds. And, *shit*, I was mean to my brother. And for what?

I rest my head on the desk and sigh. The synthesized wood is cool against my skin. I mumble to it that *I'm trying.* I mumble to it, *And for what?*

I close my work for the day.

7

I find Kieran in the den, which is where I usually find him when we're in jump space. The lights are low, letting the incandescents glow a little more brightly in the dim hues of a picture-and-video reel he's flipping through on the table. The clips and still frames fill the air above the holographic surface. They're of him and his friends from a few years ago, all in Academy attire. Pumpkin's nestled into his usual spot, completely passed out. He's always catatonic after planet-side missions. I walk right up to the bench, and he doesn't twitch. Not even a whisker.

"Hey," I say.

Kieran's hand hovers idly above the bowl of popcorn he's made. "Sup." He digs in and takes a mouthful, through which he mumbles, "Find anything good in the files?" but it sounds like *Mind anymph gud nf miles?*

Popcorn is a language I know well. I sit beside him and give Pumpkin a scratch. He rolls over to reveal his fluffy belly, slightly less orange than the rest of him. His little paws fold over in the air all cute-like, and I take the fifty-fifty chance of being mauled to rub the revealed gold mine of fluff. I am not mauled. "Standard first-contact species data. I only watched a little of the vid files, though."

"Useful?" Kieran lazily swipes a finger through the air, and the image over the table flips to the next one. It's his ex-girlfriend. She's asleep on one of the Archivist Academy Library's sofas—notably comfortable, especially during all-nighters.

They broke up when Mom...well, they broke up. I don't really know why. He gets either dismissive or inanely sarcastic about those things when I bring them up.

"We'll see," I say. "Did someone send you these?"

The question is automatic, partly because I'm tired, partly because he and I are both avoiding mentioning what a massive asshat I was earlier, but I don't need his dry, flat look to understand what a stupid question it was. It took us about seven standard months to reach this cluster via jump space. Information, though, stuff we send or broadcast through Wi-Fi on planets or through satellites to *other* planets, doesn't get the jump-space treatment. We haven't figured that out yet. The movies have, of course. Never-ending galactic civilizations where information arrives just as easily between systems as a dropped boot arrives on the floor. In reality, Kieran and I could make this trip three lifetimes over before files from home made it here. Even among systems relatively close together, courier vessels move data through jump space manually. Maybe one day we'll be high-tech like the movies, but not today.

Kieran finally flips past the picture of his ex. I think maybe the long stare and the silence are signs I should go, but Pumpkin sleepwalks into my lap and turns into a cinnamon roll, so I guess I'm stuck here forever.

Kieran passes me the popcorn. I shovel a handful in my mouth, realize I'm freaking starving, and do it again. I make monstrous snarfing sounds.

"I can put a pizza in," he says.

We've eaten exactly four pizzas since departing for our mission to the Greerant Cluster. We got them space-sealed from our favorite joint back home, but they're a luxury. Not back home, obviously. Back home they're just pizza. But out here, they aren't exactly space-efficient. We brought twelve, and even that was pushing the boundaries of a bad idea. We could have put forty Archivist-approved meal packs in place of those twelve pizzas, but nothing fixes a bad mood like pizza and, another risky luxury, beer.

"Pizza sounds great." He stands, but before he can get away, I grab his arm.

"I'm sorry," I say.

He knows exactly what for. He smiles. "It was a rough day."

"Still, I was a jerk. None of what happened was your fault."

"I know." He smiles wider, all cheeky, and maybe I want to say something a little snippy, but I don't. I'll just go for the slices with more pepperoni than the others and pretend I don't know what I'm doing. Or—I sigh—or I'll relent because he's right. And because I *was* a jerk. And because I am sorry.

I let him go, and he's gone for ten or so minutes before he comes back with an eight-slicer and a six-pack of some fruity light beer he likes. It's not my favorite, but a light buzz goes a long way in the graveyard.

When the food's done and we're each a drink in, we boot up *Smash 'Em Dead*, the best video game in the universe, and I beat his ass with a character he calls "cheap" before he switches to a character I call "broken" and beats *my* ass. Then we play co-op for a little while and beat the AI's ass together. And the AI in this game is damn good too. It's won tournaments. When this mission is over, I think I might like to spend some time at home training for one myself. Part-time professional gamer sounds my speed, even though I'm ten years senior to most full-time professional gamers. Kieran daydreams about opening a food truck sometimes while we're considering more mundane life paths. I think he'd be really good at it.

"I think I'm gonna pass out," he says. We've switched from *Smash 'Em Dead* to movies with giant robots in them. It's a whole genre.

I yawn, stretching. It feels like all the tension between us has well and truly vanished. "Me too," I say.

I clean up the wreckage from the evening—biodegradable beer cans and pizza plates and napkins and such—dumping them in the small kitchen's compost accelerator. Everything will be gooey, hydroponic, lab-ready sludge by morning, which is good because our tiny garden needs the touch-up. When I get back to the den, Kieran's snoring softly, and Pumpkin's sitting daintily on the backrest of the couch as if he's been awaiting me.

"Come on," I whisper, and we retreat to the cool interior of my cabin.

I lie in bed for a long while. I keep the lights dim and blue rather than off, because it is never as pitch-dark as on a spaceship, and as I've mentioned before, I don't love the dark. Pumpkin is purring between the wall and me, the soft rise and fall of his fur a steady comfort against my hand as his body exudes warmth against my hip. I can't sleep regardless. The silence exacerbates everything that's happened today, fuels my fears that Verity Co. is already on their way to Nebul, that there might be a cache there too, and that they might snatch it before we even have a chance to learn if there are any others among the Stelhari's worlds.

"Computer, open log," I say, because I can't stand everything being in my head. Pumpkin chirps in response and readjusts. A light goes on from my computer, accompanied by a *bloop-bloop* that means it's now recording.

"It's been a rough day," I say. "We arrived at Planet Designated 357—what the Stelhari knew as Panev—one and a half standard days ago. We picked up a signal from scanners this morning. There was a tier-one cache, but Verity Co. arrived and..." I trail off, already exhausted by the retelling. I'm quiet for a long time, but the recording won't stop until I tell it to. "I thought about Mom today." I steady my breath. "And I hung out with Kieran. And Pumpkin. We played *Smash 'Em Dead*. It was...okay. Good. Good on its own, but with the whole failed excavation thing, just okay."

I don't know who I'm talking to. Myself? I feel stupid for starting the log in the first place. Who would listen to this? Will *I* listen to this, years from now?

"We had another one of the pizzas," I blurt out anyway. "It was also good."

I'm talking in circles, and I hate myself. If a future archeologist ever finds this, they'll mark me under *mundanities* and bury my data deep in a bin. I stop the recording. Sometimes I wonder why I do anything or if anything I do matters.

I think about deleting the log right then and there, but I don't, and I don't know why.

8

When I was a kid, I watched a lot of movies about space travel. Even though it was part of our everyday life, directors still found ways to make the concept fantastical and adventurous. Alien civilizations, space monsters, utopian garden planets touched by the gods. Even contrasted with the reality of interstellar travel and cosmic work, I entered into the Archivists with a lot of fantastical notions about what space and ship life would be like. But I have to say, as alluring as the movies are with their action and romance and constant adventure, there sure is a lot of downtime. It's like life planet-side but on a thing shooting through the stars.

I eat breakfast with Kieran on the couch a little later than usual. He's eating hot cereal agonizingly slowly, sucking on the spoon between bites. He's staring transfixed at the show we're watching. Just *suck suck suck*.

"Kieran," I say. "Stop."

"Stop what?"

"Smacking."

He frowns. "I'm not smacking."

"Dude. Yes you are."

"Whatever," he says, but the sucking ceases.

I have to change out a recycling filter. It's the worst chore on the ship because if you slip up, you kill everyone. Luckily, it needs changing only once every six standard months, but here we are. I disengage one of the two filters, the spent one, from the locks keeping it in place in the filtration vent.

BWAH.

That's the sound of the death alarm.

BWAH.

It is accompanied by a terrifying crimson light. The builders of this ship decided it was the color most likely to make a crewmate shit themselves in an emergency.

BWAH.

"Kieran!" I start to warn, but he's already sprinting across the den, leaping over the couches. Pumpkin is hot on his tail. Cats also shit themselves at flashing crimson lights. "I just forgot to—"

They disappear into the cockpit before I can finish.

"Damn it," I say.

BWAH.

I hoist the new clean filter and begin locking it into place, mumbling about chores and alarms and promises to pin any cat-shit duty on Kieran because he's the tech guy and this is his niche, but no, here I am, messing everything up.

BWAooorp.

The lights go off with the dying klaxon because a filter is back in place now. I come off the ladder, and Kieran and Pumpkin are waiting for me by the couches, deadpan.

"Don't," I say.

"See?" Kieran looks so proud. "See how easy it is to forget to engage diagnosis protocols?"

"Kieran. Seriously."

Last time, he decided to change the filter at an ungodly hour and forgot to tell the ship something critical was about to be removed, albeit temporarily. The *BWAH*s were going off, the lights were flashing, and I was pulled from REM right into hell, and half-drugged-up on cold medicine to boot. I lectured him for six days.

Now he's smiling like an idiot. "Seriously what? Seriously hard to remember, right?"

"Stop."

"You owe me a lifetime of pizza!" He stalks me to dead-electronics storage. "That was the deal! *I'd never forget, Kieran,"* he says, mocking me. *"I'd buy you a lifetime of pizza if I was so stupid I forgot!"*

"Fine! Okay! We get universe-saving information from this cluster, and then we go home and I buy you so much pizza you smack it all down and kill yourself."

"You know what I think?"

"I don't care."

"I think you're a sore loser."

I'm listening to music in my cabin with the door open, snoozing on the rug.

"Meow."

Pumpkin's come in, and *oh, big stretch.* "Hey, buddy."

His pupils dilate to soulless orbs, and he attacks my face.

Kieran and I build Pumpkin an obstacle course of blankets, pillows, and various mechanical enhancements, because Pumpkin has attacked my face. He is pent up. We run him through blanket hoops and pillow forts with a green laser beam. He runs and jumps so fast and far that sometimes he's airborne for nearly three seconds. He announces that he is satisfied by unceremoniously flopping over onto his side. We give him scratchies and tell him he's a warrior while he purrs.

It's late at night. Pumpkin's been in a coma since the

obstacle course. He's curled into a nook on my desk, a little square of space I keep clear just for him. Kieran's gone to bed too, in his cabin this time. Tomorrow we're due to land on Nebul, and because of this I can't bring myself to close my eyes.

After a handful of hours tossing and turning, I sit at my desk. Pumpkin shifts a little as the holographic emitter activates, and the empty floor space fills with Blyreena's presence.

9

Recording Playback 1.0023.498.x

Speaker and Authorizer: Organizer President, Interstel Councilmember Sy. Blyreena Ekstafor

Rotation 2, Mayak Harvest, 3550

I met Ovlan long before he was significant to me. We both enrolled in the Capital Academy's Civil Service advanced degree program the same year, and though my interest was administration and organization, and his was city and habitat design, we found ourselves in the same cohort. I knew his name; we chatted at luncheons and waved to each other in the hall, but ultimately, I found our meetings and conversations—as well as him, himself—to be unremarkable. We only ever had core classes together, and of them, only two in year one. By year two I hardly saw him at all. We were no longer neophytes in the program, and I was caught up in my thesis, he in his.

Our third and final year brought with it some of the most significant stresses of my life. I was traveling all over the capital, conducting interviews with small-time and prominent Organizers alike, as well as a number of councilpeople from Interstel, the government body on which my ambitions were ultimately set. My research targeted the cultural tendency for artificial division along political lines, and how our capital's vehemently split parties could be extrapolated to highlight the divisive issues facing Interstel and the myriad colonies it attempted to govern. My proposition was a "common goals first" policy that built bridges instead of burned them. I was naïve, oh yes, but some things, I thought—and I still do think—are worth being naïve for.

Toward the end of the year, I had gathered my evidence and propositions into a nearly sixty-quadrabyte multimedia presentation, which I had rehearsed a hundred times—almost literally, but not quite—before presenting to the Academy review board.

Three out of the four reviewers gave me passing marks, the requisite number to graduate from the program many weeks later. But the fourth who didn't provided, well...to call it a scathing review would be beneath the individual's penchant for cruelty. It devastated me, that review. My thesis had been the heart and soul of my hope for unification across the stars, for an end to the cold wars keeping necessary supplies from the most disadvantaged colonies, for an end to the soul-sucking reality of fifty billion of our own people not getting what they needed to live even a simple, comfortable life because of century-old grudges and greed. I would graduate, yes, but I could not steer my mind away from the negative. We're told not to take criticism of our work personally, but really, who has ever managed that?

I could focus on that review and nothing else, and in my addled state I accomplished something quite embarrassing. Through a veil of tears, I drove my personal dual-hover transport right into another vehicle—one that was parked, mind you—not ten seconds after powering on. The quad-hover whose power supply I crushed was Ovlan's.

He had been walking into the garage when it happened. He ran right over, and his first words, the first sounds to cut through my panic, were: "Wow, great aim!"

He knelt and examined the damage to his transport, noting the small crushed casing on the underside I'd managed to scoop under and destroy. The front of my dual-hover was also crushed.

When he looked up from the damage, he asked, "Are you okay?" He was smiling. *Smiling.* Not glowering, or snarling, or pacing about in a frustrated rage—like I might have done, if someone had hit my innocuous transport parked neatly in the lines. He was such a beautiful soul; you could hardly imagine such a person could exist. He exuded kindness like a sun does warmth.

"I'm so sorry," I told him.

"No problem," he said. "No problem." He ended up being the one to call a repair service. He called in both our wrecks. When he hung up, he looked at me and asked again, "So, are you okay?"

I couldn't believe how nice he was being, and, in hindsight, I can't believe how badly I took advantage of his niceness. I don't know if it was his kind face, our being peers, or my having had a terribly awful day, but I told him the full extent of my not being okay. The floodgates had opened. I talked until the repair crew came. When they arrived, Ovlan mentioned there was a place for drinks nearby. We went, and he listened to me talk about my thesis for hours. When I was done and a little loopy from the fizz, I felt awful.

"I'm sorry," I told him. "I've taken up so much of your time."

He shrugged, waved the concern away. It was a very *Ovlan* thing to do. "You've taken nothing that I have not offered."

He'd listened so intently, smiled ruefully at my confessions and doubts, scoffed at my reenactments of certain reviewers. I showed him the bad review in the end. Just the final paragraph on the written remarks, just the one that had really got to me and curdled my resolve into tears enough to crash a transport:

An unabashed journey in naïveté, forming a singular utter lack of any understanding about the Organizers, Interstel, and their mission. It is my absolute recommendation that this individual not only cease their study and switch to a more suitable field—perhaps fiction-writing for children—but that to hire them into a position anywhere near the Organizers would be parallel to a criminal act.

Ovlan stared at it for a long time. He laughed, which worried me—hurt me—but he patched the wound right up, shook his head, smiled, and said, "What an idiot."

Even though I know to expect it, leaving jump space startles me. There's a moment, when a ship leaves behind the pretty lights for blackness and dotted stars, where the whole thing rumbles worse than a dinghy breaking atmosphere. The light outside dims, and everything seems darker. I never feel as much like I've gone to another world as when this happens.

I get a notification from my brother: *Iari system, ho!*

That's good news, but… I sigh at Blyreena paused before me. I don't know what she's trying to tell me. I don't know what any of this has to do with what destroyed countless civilizations, or a last stand against it. I want to stay and listen to everything, but I'm fried again. I'm frustrated and a little exhausted. I'm hoping that we pick up signs of any cache quickly so that I can shift my focus to finding something with meaning. I sigh again and close the recording, saving my place, and head for the cockpit.

"How goes the data-diving?" Kieran asks as I arrive.

I scoop Pumpkin out of my seat and put him on my lap once I've sat, but he's affronted and hops to the floor. "I don't know," I say, still deep in thought about the whole thing.

Ahead of us, growing larger with each moment, is our target destination, the planet Blyreena sent Panev's top scientists to: Nebul. It's the size of a small marble at the moment, gray as a storm cloud, cut through with ravines like deep, bloodless cuts. "In the recording, she's just talking about her life."

"Isn't that what most caches have? Diaries, records, those kinds of things you archeologists like?"

"Yeah. But most caches don't start with a recording proclaiming they know what's destroying them and that they have a solution to it." Pumpkin jumps back into my lap, preferring pets to his pride and the cold steel against his toe beans. "I just..." I feel bad, but say, small-like, "...thought she might get straight to the point."

"But there were other data modules that weren't completed in the copy, right?"

"Yeah."

Kieran nods like he's resolved himself to do something. "Those probably had the information you're looking for."

"Information *we're* looking for," I remind him.

"You know what I mean."

We watch the approaching planet for a while. It won't be long before we lock into orbit and can begin our scan. Hopefully, we find something fast, because odds are if Verity Co. listened to Blyreena enough to know about the science team's trajectory, they're already here. I cross my fingers that they didn't listen. I cross my toes that they just went home.

There's no news tonight.

When I wake up the next morning, there's still none. The scanners are churning, doing their unbearably slow but necessary work. Pacing does little to calm my nerves, so it's back to task with what I have. I sit once again in my cabin and pick up with Blyreena where she left off.

10

Recording Playback 1.0023.498.x

Speaker and Authorizer: Organizer President, Interstel Councilmember Sy. Blyreena Ekstafor

Rotation 2, Mayak Harvest, 3550

That pseudotherapy session in the bar with Ovlan became the first of many dates. We never truly called them such, never treated our outings between then and graduation as particularly romantic. It was almost an accident, us falling in love. We liked many of the same things: industrial flute jazz, gardening, cooking elaborate meals, *eating* elaborate meals, and of course, good shows. But who among us doesn't, really? Our favorites were comedies and cooking shows, and in a rare spark of genius, both genres blended into one, a daring amalgamation we rewatched many times throughout our happy relationship.

But we weren't only couch potatoes, good jokesters, and foodies. We both shared a deep admiration for the work of the Organizers and the various departments they umbrella. Ovlan of course held a deep passion for the Builders. As a child living in the rural zones outside the capital, Builder-operations funding was the only reason he and his mother had clean water, tenable soil, and a warm home to protect against Panev's harshest elements. In ages past, our poorest city-states were left on their own come droughts or frost, but decades ago a particularly forward-thinking Builder President commissioned the Rural Habitat Improvement Effort, a coalition driven not by capital politicians, but by city-state leadership. Inflated with funds and resources, Ovlan's remote home flourished with the installation of bolstered soils and terraforming turf, artificial water lines and a complete weather-shielding grid. As he put it, Builder intervention changed the lives of him and his one thousand and eleven neighbors nearly overnight.

I led a rather different life.

My father was in the Interstel Navy and was honored for discovering six exoplanets, one previously inhabited and, though we wouldn't know for decades, destroyed by Endri. He was honorably discharged when an airlock malfunction caused one of his lungs to collapse.

This was well before he and my dad, who worked with the Educators, adopted me. The two of them moved in together a month after the accident, my dad more than happy to care for him. Between my dad's generous Educator salary and my father's military stipend, we managed a very happy life.

Father's duty and honor were instilled in me early. He had an enormous passion and respect for life—one of the tenets, in fact, of the Interstel Navy, though I think he had the heart of it long before he signed up. Once, I found a refuse crawler in my room, big as my six-year-old hand. I screamed and picked up a doll's crest iron (even then, I was a diva), raising it to strike—several times if I had to.

Father came in and stayed my hand. "Bly," he said to me. "You want to kill this?"

It was an odd question. Did I *want* to kill the crawler? I wanted it gone, that was certain. It was spindly, with eighteen legs and a chitinous little mouth that made me want to scream again.

But as scary as it was—as horrifying and inStelhari as it was—Father found a glass and captured it, put his hand—bare and exposed!—right over the top to keep it inside, and told me to come with him to the patio.

"There were many times on other worlds," he said, speaking slowly. He always spoke slowly, taking long, purposeful breaths between every handful of words, and somehow this made everything he said seem wise. Each word was an effort, something that *had* to be said. "When I was scared," he went on. "I would see a shadow or a flicker and want to raise my weapon. But I was honor-bound to stay my hand. We were strangers on those planets. Whether bug, or plant, or small creature...we were the intruders. And we wanted to treat them with respect."

He nodded his head to the patio, and I touched the sensor to open it. The sounds of the capital, I remember them so clearly. So stunningly, impossibly clearly. I have few such clear memories of youth. The ambient laughing and conversation, small figures walking around the lake; the faint smell of wildflowers in season, blooming beneath the Sciences Spire; and its cooling shadow cast across our apartment like a shield from the sun.

My father followed me out onto the patio. "In those moments of fear of other creatures, it was always important to look for the similarities. Do you know what the greatest thing we have in common with alien flora and fauna is? What the greatest thing you have in common with this bug is?"

I looked at the bug. Indeed, so like an alien. "Bleh!" I think I said.

My father chuckled and coughed. "Try."

The bug was squirming in the glass. It had barely enough space for its legs, and I kept fearing it would bite my father's hand. It didn't. "It has legs," I said, and Father smiled and nodded, encouraging me to keep going. "Eyes, too. And…it doesn't like being trapped. I wouldn't want to be in a glass."

"Why doesn't it like being trapped?"

"It's scared," I said, like a revelation.

My father took his hand off the glass, angled it out over the lake and crowds below. The creature inside scuttled eagerly out, unfurled its iridescent wings, and flew off with a buzzing clamor. It was rather clumsy in the air, bobbing almost cutely. But don't get me wrong. Refuse crawlers are savage little things.

"Life," my father said, "is what we have the most in common with every other creature. We all want to live and we become scared when living is threatened. All of us just want to survive and be comfortable, be happy."

The bug faded to a brown dot, then vanished into a blooming tree.

Years later, I knew Ovlan was someone special

when after a night we'd spent together close to graduation, I heard him scream from his kitchen. It was a tight, bloodcurdling thing, and I thought maybe he'd cut himself badly making a romantic breakfast (turned out, he was never the sort, but we got on). I rushed to the kitchen and found him on the countertop, clutching a cabinet knob for dear life, staring down at the floor and screaming, "I let you live, you let me live! Deal? Deal?"

He was hysterical, and I had to scour the floor very carefully to find what had set him off: a snake. A tiny sliver of a thing, no longer than the length of my finger. I don't think it had even noticed Ovlan. When I saw this, I burst out laughing. I could not stop. The sight of this sweet, boisterous man pinched onto the counter, screeching over a garden hisser, a thing he must have seen a million times living in the fields and plains. He could have poked it with his toe and the thing would have died, and instead he was making a soul pact with it.

"Bly!" he cried, more scared than indignant. "Don't lose sight of it!" As if it were some scuttler drone and not a tiny, harmless thing.

I eventually recovered and, though I am not a fan of invading crawling entities either, managed to get the thing outside safely. In a way, it reminded me of that beautiful morning with my father and the refuse crawler.

Ovlan came down from the countertop with a look of deep shame. "Is our relationship over?"

"Depends," I said. "Did the snake seal the pact while I was laughing at you?"

"No, else I might have agreed to get back on the floor."

"Well, I guess I'll keep you then." We kissed, and from then on I was very careful about never showing him anything interesting about snakes.

Just kidding.

I teased him about it all the time. We graduated a week and a half later and, not being able to help myself, I got him one of those trick cylinders with the springy confetti inside. I specifically ordered the one where the large springy was a snake. He didn't break up with me then, so I knew he probably wouldn't ever.

Graduated, we could hardly wait to put what we had learned into action. After a modest celebration with our families, we retreated to my apartment and filled out job applications until the early hours of the next day. You could say that we were kind of nerds. But both of our lives had been shaped by Interstel, by the Organizers, by the Builders and Educators and Financers, and all the other wings of our people's leadership. We wanted desperately to give back, and to help shape the world.

Ovlan—smart, caring, ingenious, lovable Ovlan—

he got a job with the Builders ten days after graduating. We celebrated at our favorite restaurant. We got high on fizz and, while high on fizz, literally shouted from the rooftops with joy. He had made it, and in him making it, *I* had made it. And I knew my time was coming soon. Ovlan and I both knew that not long after his own victory, mine would come.

But it didn't.

I heard nothing the week after Ovlan's hiring, or the week after that. Ovlan started his new job and left me with a squeeze of the hand and a promise something would come in soon. He worked a week, two weeks, a month. Two months. Three. All the applications I'd submitted, all the energy I'd given, and *nothing*. I was so terrified, more than I'd ever been in my life, that I had failed. That I was a failure.

A notification interrupts and pauses the recording automatically, leaving Blyreena a distressed hologram in the air, reliving the trauma of her failure. Was this the face I made when Verity Co. took that cache from us?

I click a button to answer the open line to the cockpit. "Scout," Kieran says. "Scans have found something. There's another cache here."

11

We're flying over a district dotted evenly in stout, squat buildings, a few kilometers beneath which rests the cache Kieran picked up on the orbital scanners. We couldn't pick up any other ships in orbit or boots on the ground, just like on Panev, but now that we know Verity Co. is in this cluster, we don't expect to. Even if they were right in front of us, we don't expect to. Their stealth technology is the best home has to offer and is reserved for their operatives alone. If they're here, we'll just have to work around them to get to the cache. It's a likelihood I've psyched myself up for.

The planet below, Nebul, looks very different from Panev. On Panev, we flew into a guarded, central area of an expansive urban zone touched with wide and frequent plots of unpaved nature. Impressive sky-reaching architecture was distinct even from the atmosphere. Here, nature is entirely overlaid with steel and plasticrete. The city below stretches from horizon to horizon, a perfectly manufactured grid of straight lines and evenly spaced properties, most of which stand a single story high. Given the sun's proximity and the coordinates of the cache, I find myself wondering—and noting, in my suit's internal computer—if the Stelhari on this planet spent much of their time underground.

Kieran leans over the dash closer to the front-facing window. "Hey, is that—"

"Shit," I say, because we see them at the same time: the two Verity Co. grunts in their sleek, *V*-marked uniforms, fussing over the partly broken steel double doors of an impressive-looking building. Impressive-looking because among a sea of single-story, block-shaped structures, it stands three stories tall with a domed roof.

One of the grunts, the guy, looks up at us just as Kieran is trying to veer out of sight. "Shit," I say again.

"Maybe they didn't see us."

"They saw us." I go to rub my temples but touch my helmet instead. Doesn't have quite the same effect. "Nothing to do but land."

"Are you sure?" There's a slight whine in Kieran's tone, a high note of worry. Pumpkin echoes him with a yowl of his own, but I think it's because he's tired of the straps keeping him in his seat.

"We have to," I say.

I'm stressed too. I'm worried too. I don't want to get shot or watch my brother or my cat get shot, but if Verity Co. is already busting down a door… I look at the locked-in coordinates for the cache on the dashboard. It's underground, pretty much right below us—right below *them*.

"What are you going to do?" Kieran asks warily, like he thinks I might ask him to ram them with our dinghy. He's activated the underside thrusters, lowering us onto a patch of flat road not far from the doors Verity Co. is trying to break down. Or, *was* trying to break down. The grunts are walking our way now.

"We have to make them see reason."

The landers meet plasticrete, the engine powers down, and Kieran lets Pumpkin out of his seat. I push open the hatch to a pair of guns pointed at us. Even prepared for it, my breath catches. Those weapons are lethal, their wielders soulless, and I'm standing here having to persuade what is essentially stone to be… something nicer and more personable than stone.

"Whoa! Hey!" Kieran puts his hands up. Pumpkin hops down from his strapped prison and rolls along the floor. "Don't shoot!"

"Best close that hatch and fly back up to space," the woman says. She's smirking. "And we won't."

"Have you found the cache?" My voice comes out even despite the rib-rattling heartbeat.

"That's not really your concern right now, is it? Given I'm pointing a gun at you and the only thing that will stop me pulling the trigger is if you close that door and go back to orbit."

"Shame to die so far from home," the guy says. His smirk matches hers. Confident and demeaning, like bullies in a schoolyard. That's basically what Verity Co. is. Bullies in a schoolyard, where the schoolyard's all the universe.

I hold in a frustrated sigh. "Just hear us out."

"No," the woman says.

"Fine. Then shoot me."

"Scout!" I can practically hear Kieran's jaw drop, can feel his eyes widen to burn a hole in the back of my head.

Pumpkin pads in from behind me and winds himself through my legs. He sits between my feet and stares up at the Verity grunts like, *Yeah, what are you gonna do, shoot me?*

The man fires.

I scream; Kieran screams; Pumpkin screams. He retreats from the shot's small crater ten centimeters from where his little booted paw had touched this world's pavement.

"Holy shit!" Kieran cries.

"You'd shoot a cat?" I yell. My arms are over my head, as if that would save me from a bullet.

Pumpkin is in the cockpit screaming for us to ascend.

"Of course not. That was a warning," the definitely supervillain-wannabe growls, but maybe *this* is where I've got them cornered—finally—because his partner looks, for a moment, starkly surprised that he fired at all. "Next one's through your head."

"Scout," Kieran begs. "Let's just go."

"Ma-meow!" Pumpkin cries. "Ma-meow!" *Ascend! Ascend!*

"You two can go," I say and take a step off the dinghy.

There's a very real moment where the man's face goes deadpan, and his gun shifts, and I am certain I'm going to die, but then the woman puts her hand to his weapon and forces it—softly—down. "What a little idiot you are," she tells me.

"The cache you stole details what happened to this cluster, what might have happened to every dead civilization we've ever come across. They *knew*."

"Great. Sounds like pay dirt." But she sniffs, looks left, puts her tongue in her cheek. She cares. Even if it's just a tiny, infinitesimal amount of empathy, it's there. I just *know* it. I'm not good with tech or weapons or heights or goodbyes, but I *know* people. It's my job to know them.

I take a breath. "If you take it to Verity Co.—"

"If? *If?*" She laughs, pretty and cruel. "We're taking the cache home, kid."

"*Kid?* Seriously?" I can't stop a smirk. Going by looks—though you can't always tell, especially with Verity Co.—we're the same age.

"Oh please," the woman says. She's all sneers now, no flicker of empathy to be found. "Your asinine daydreamer's gig with the Archivists says all anyone needs to know about your maturity. We're taking this and any other cache in this cluster, and we're bringing them to Verity Co. You've lost. Go home."

I think a moment. "No."

The man groans. "June, just shoot them."

The woman, June, I guess, scoffs. She's squinting her eyes; her lips are just slightly twitching out of reflex. Telepathy. The man is squinting too.

"June," I say, "I'm Scout. And this is my brother, Kieran, and our cat, Pumpkin." (*Ascend!*) "I know it's your job to shop the cosmos for your masters"—I get a viper's glare at this—"but both our homes' safety is in very real danger. We've been searching for years for some sign of what destroyed all these civilizations, something beyond the Remnants, and now we've found a cache that details a last stand and a working knowledge of—"

June puts her hand up. It's such a cutting gesture that I stop talking immediately.

"You can scour this planet if you want," she says, "but the cache is ours. Come any closer to the main building than this and we *will* shoot."

Main building. I flick my eyes over their shoulders toward the building with the partially busted doors and the Stelhari Organizer's emblem above them.

"Hey." She snaps her fingers to draw my gaze back to her narrowed eyes. "I'm serious. Do you understand?"

"Why can't—"

"This is professionalism, Scout." I guess she was listening to what I was saying, at least partly. "We're not friends. We're not chums. We're two organizations after the same prize, and like usual, yours has fallen short."

"Scout," Kieran warns, but I can't keep my mouth shut. I just don't get it.

"Why even work for those assholes?" is all I can manage. Why can't they see the value in the thing they're taking? Why can't they see what Verity Co. would, or wouldn't, do with it?

"Because this is the real world." June holsters her

gun. "Make the right call for your brother and your… this is not an appropriate environment for a cat."

"He likes it," Kieran mumbles, but Pumpkin has not stopped yowling.

She gives my brother a look like he's diseased and highly contagious, then shakes her head and retreats back to the building. The Organizer's office. Her partner trails after her, but unlike her, he keeps his gun out. He looks back at us a few times, seemingly willing and eager to use it. After a little while, when we don't follow, he touches June's shoulder. They share a derisive laugh.

I watch them all the way up the steps. June starts examining the doors while the guy plucks six black spheres from his belt and throws them into the air. They float a moment, disperse, and then a sheen of translucence slips over them like a wave, turning them invisible.

Sensor drones. They'd really shoot us if we got close. They really would.

I sit down on the cracked plasticrete.

"Hey." Kieran sits next to me, and Pumpkin, who has stopped screaming, sits next to him. "You tried."

"I failed."

My brother sighs and puts an arm around my shoulders, bopping his helmet to mine once. "It's Verity Co. Let's just go."

I make a frustrated sound in my throat. It wants to turn into a remark that he's wrong, that we can still get to the cache first, but it fizzles into nothing but a tired huff of air.

12

I can't be convinced to leave. Kieran has tried a few times now, but even though I know it's futile, I won't board the dinghy. We traveled months to get here. We stumbled blindly into answers, but they're answers all the same, answers to the most important questions in the universe.

June and her accomplice have taken to bashing the door in with small, powerful robots. It looks like long work. They're a hundred meters away, but every now and then the faint white light of the sun catches the reinforced glass of their helmets looking our way.

When I can't stand their and Kieran's and Pumpkin's stares, I retreat to where I've found a patch of hidden, dry, and lifeless dirt beneath where a road bunched up and crumbled. It is such a small patch. I plant the seeds and dump the water. I hope Kieran's not watching. I want to be alone. The bunched road, cinched together into a pyramid over the dirt, provides me some cover from Verity Co. at least.

I can't stand them. I can't stand what they do. I can't stand their hollow reasoning. This cluster had the potential to be one of the greatest, most significant discoveries in our history, and now Blyreena and her people's work will be locked behind an interminable paywall or, if deemed too valuable to sell, kept for Verity Co.'s self-propagating uses alone. I shake with rage that our home worlds might be under threat from whatever wiped everyone else out, and that the Verity Co.'s of the world are content to ignore that possibility—that *likelihood*—for a profit. I want to scream, I'm so frustrated.

I walk back to my brother. He hasn't left where he was sitting beside me about an hour ago.

I follow his gaze to the Organizer's office, where June is squeezing herself inside the removed doors. She steps out and sends a robot inside after a minute, probably to clear more of a path. I wish all those little bots would break down without repair. I will it like I might honest-to-cosmos develop powers right here, but lo. You know how it goes. I can't even pull from the dark, sad well within myself and blow up their dinghy so they can't get back to their ship, because I have no idea where it is, and our scanners can't pick up something stealthed as effectively as theirs must be.

"Hey," Kieran finally says. Pumpkin's in his lap and getting lots of pets.

I sit next to them. "Hey."

"Looks like they're getting inside."

"Yeah."

Harsh light fills the dark spaces behind the doors, Verity Co.'s silhouettes moving like lithe shadows between the rubble. The robots' grinding, crunching work echoes off the buildings all around us.

"I wonder how they found it so fast," Kieran says.

"Verity Co." Like that in itself is the reason. And it kind of is. Top-of-the-line resources, singular ethics, skilled cache-hunters upgraded with bionics and platinum-grade cybernetics...

"Even Verity Co. can't have orbital scanners that see through fortified earth and steel."

The ping we got on the cache from orbit was indeed from underground, from a location whose very purpose must have been amplifying the signal in otherwise impassable conditions. It's as clear to me as it must be to the Verity grunts that there are underground structures, but as far as I know, Kieran's right. Only seismic imaging could really map things that deep. We have the location of the cache but not the path there. "They probably have a seismic reader here," I say.

"Hm. No. I don't think so."

I'm not arguing with the tech kid.

"Even if they had it, they'd have to have been here during a quake to get those kinds of reads," he says.

"Tremor-pulse scanner then." I know *some* stuff.

He shakes his head. "We'd see it if they had it. Things are big and unwieldy as all hell."

The lights and silhouettes move deeper inside the Organizer's office, almost out of sight. I'd admire the building more if not for its inhabitants. Geometric, aesthetic carvings in the walls, filled in with reflective glass, catch the sun so that its light pools into the cracks like neon. The dome shines too, a bright beacon in the otherwise drab, dusty terrain. Even though the whole planet is a grid of buildings mapped along identical plots and straight lines, there is something very central about it. Tall, bright, and decorated, it draws the eye.

It reminds me of the dilapidated spire on Panev. The Organizers really lucked out with the working digs. Only...the spire wasn't for that arm of the Stelhari government.

I think real hard for a moment.

"Do you think," I whisper, because I cannot risk even the zero percent chance Verity Co. can hear me, "maybe they don't know how to get to the cache? Maybe they're just guessing?"

Pumpkin rolls over to reveal his suited belly. Kieran keeps petting. "Doubt it."

I push to a stand and start toward our dinghy.

He calls after me, "Are we going?"

"Shh," I snap, and wave for him to follow.

"What?"

"Just—come on, Kieran. Please."

He picks Pumpkin up and follows me to the dinghy, where I look over the scan we picked up from orbit. The red blip that marks the cache rests five kilometers beneath the ground we're parked on, angled slightly more east, a few meters away from being directly below the Organizer's office. It is reasonable to think that it is, therefore, connected to the Organizer's office. Pure proximity. And no other building—

I inhale sharply.

"What?" Kieran's pressed to me, shoulder to shoulder, Pumpkin held close to his chest so we can all get a look at the small screen on the dash.

"It's the biggest," I blurt. I giggle. It sounds mad, probably.

"What?"

"They think the path underground is in the Organizer's office because it's the *biggest* building. The *main* building."

"What's that have to do with anything?"

I close the scan data. "On Panev, we found the cache

in the most impressive building, right?" Kieran's looking at me like I've become slightly deranged, but Pumpkin's tail is flicking. He's got it too, I think. "But it was the Sciences Spire. Blyreena called it that. It's where the scientists worked, not the Organizers."

"Organizers are like..."

"Like, purely administrivia; coordinating projects between other wings of government; public liaisons," I ramble. I know I'm not making sense to him. It's alright in my head, but it never comes out the way it sounds in my head. "Point is, Verity Co. is"—I look out the hatch to make sure they haven't snuck up on us—"assuming the cache will be there because it's the biggest, most impressive building."

I walk slowly out the hatch, trying to maintain my look of defeat from before. Lights and shadow still dance just inside the doors of the Organizer's office, and the din of robots is still echoing off the grid.

"That's it?" Kieran sighs. "Scout, I don't know. This sounds like reaching."

I laugh. It *is* ludicrous to think that they'd make such a banal mistake, but not when everything they've seen supports it. The cache is pinging from right below the office, and the last planet's cache was nestled right into the heart of the biggest, obviously most central structure in the city. Even back home, the most important secrets always end up in the most imposing constructions: Verity Co.'s headquarters, for one; along with all the big intersystem banks that hold our home's wealth; museums; academies... The bigger something is the more important it is, we've all seemed to agree. It's like everyone's forgotten that the hallmark discovery for nuclear power came from a dead exoplanet with an estimated former population of just five hundred thousand native Espilie people.

The cache on Panev was in the *Sciences* Spire. Blyreena was sending *scientists* to Nebul, not Organizers. I don't understand the Stelhari government perfectly, the intricacies of how each branch supported the other, but I've listened enough to know that if the cache was in the science-dedicated building on Panev, it'll be in the science-dedicated building here too.

I lead the way to the closest building that's not the Organizer's office and search the exterior for any sign of its purpose.

"Wait," Kieran says. He's frowning. "Why wouldn't they be right?"

There's nothing marking the outside, but the flimsy door gives easily, revealing a dusty, rubble-filled room beyond. An emblem and a word are engraved into the wall, cut through by a crack. My suit's computer translates it to *Builders*.

"Because I think the cache initiative belonged to

the Sciences, not the Organizers," I say, picking up the pace to the next building.

"Wasn't that what, uh, that Stelhari was, though? An Organizer?"

"Blyreena? She was an Organizer, yeah, but also Panev's president and an Interstel councilmember."

"So?" He drags the word out, confused.

"So we're looking for the Sciences building, I think." I hope.

I push my way into another blocky structure to see a foreign symbol denoting the Stelhari currency and a word below it translating to *Financers*. My hunch about this area was right, at least. It seems like, while all the buildings on Nebul are practically identical, the ones around the Organizer's office are all dedicated to a wing of the Stelhari government. I'm too invested to distract myself with wondering about the geographical and cultural differences that led to such different prioritizations in construction between Panev and Nebul, but I make a note to look into it later.

Another building takes a little longer to get into, but when I do, I find *Educators* along the back wall. Kieran's picked up the gist of it now. He helps me discover buildings dedicated to the Navy, Transportation, Histories, and Ethics. We're half a kilometer away from our dinghy now, but I'm moving with purpose—not tired at all. I'm giddy with the possibility that I'm right, that Verity Co.'s blunt tactics have finally failed them, that their inability to see this civilization as once alive has failed them. But I'm nervous too. If I'm wrong, I'll be devastated.

We arrive at another building the size and shape of all the others, with a dark, dusty foyer I glimpse through a fissure in the outside wall. I run my headlamp over the interior, highlighting what symbols I can find. My translator displays the half-crumbled letters *Scien* above a parabolic emblem of an atom. I sigh with relief.

"Let's find a way in," I say, and I'm breathless with the hope of it.

13

The Sciences building is almost pitch-dark inside once we've figured out how to get in (through the ceiling, big surprise). We've dropped into a mostly empty foyer with a wide central desk, much like in every other structure, and a few dilapidated benches along the walls near the crumbled front door. Their cushions have deteriorated entirely, leaving strings of polyfiber and the ash of what might have become mold if this planet allowed for any sort of life at all.

It's quiet in addition to the dark. Pumpkin's delicate little steps go unheard as he scampers over benches, rubble, and desks, his headlight whipping around the place like a light show.

"Come on, buddy." I try to snatch him up, but he

skids over a patch of dusty tile and darts toward a square passage into a narrow hallway.

Kieran and I go after him. The hall has a low ceiling, and the stairs Pumpkin has found are decayed and scuffed, with rubble partly blocking their sharp angle downward. *Downward.* Underground. I let out a breath like a nervous lightjetter before a race, and Pumpkin meows.

"You were right," Kieran says.

"Maybe." My chest is tight, but I start on the stairs, maneuvering around the portion of wall that's collapsed onto them. Pumpkin, out of exploratory greed or fear of me picking him up, skitters down into the dark ahead of me, his lamp revealing the barren floor below. "We shouldn't get our hopes up."

But my hopes are up. They're way up. My heart is pounding in an anxious, excited rhythm, and my face hurts from alternating between a giddy smile and a deep, doubtful frown. As hopeful as I am, I'm also terrified.

If I am right, and Verity Co. is wrong, they'll come for us. Now I realize I've done nothing to hide our tracks. Do I say something? Do I let Kieran go alone, or—

"Look." Kieran's arrived on the basement floor beside me, pointing to a reinforced steel door without a handle. Even the wall is reinforced with armored steel.

A dull painted banner across the metal spells out in an alien language that only elite personnel are allowed inside. "Think this is it?"

"It's not exactly kilometers underground." But maybe. Maybe it is. Pumpkin sniffs at the base of the door, prowling its length.

"But it could lead there." An edge of boyish excitement slips into Kieran's voice. He approaches the door, considering it, touching it, tracing the grooves and testing for cracks. He stops at some kind of card reader on the frame, but it doesn't activate at his touch. "Gonna need a few minutes."

"Okay." I look back to the stairs. "I'm going to see if I can cover our tracks." That, and I can't bear to stand and watch, holding my breath for whatever's on the other side of that steel.

Kieran doesn't answer. He's already lost in the puzzle of how to open a thousand-year-old, electronically locked door without power.

Pumpkin follows me back upstairs, probably because the door problem isn't very fun for him either. Cats, like most people, have no idea how to use alien electronics.

We get back to the foyer. The single thin sliver of light that makes it through the ceiling is fainter now. Nebul is spinning slowly away from its system's sun, turning toward night. There's no wind, but the cord we anchored and came down on is wavering with the weight of the descender on its end—sure proof we've been here.

"Looks like de-anchoring is the best option," I say, mostly to myself, but Pumpkin too, I guess.

He sits in the halo of light near the cord and licks his lips at me. He does not intend to help, but lucky for me I don't need it. The descender can go back along the line and disconnect the anchor at the top. It'll make a clatter on the way down, but so long as no one is too close, only me and Pumpkin will hear it.

So long as no one is too close.

I grimace and attach the descender to my belt. "Be right back, buddy."

The gear pulls me swiftly up the line with a pleasant *zzzzzziiipppp*. The darkening air is still stagnant at the top, though growing cooler. It's quiet, too, like the silence inside the Sciences building evaporated out into the larger world while we were inside it. It's unnerving, given the ambient noise of robots and drones that has permeated the empty streets since our arrival.

I look out over the destroyed civilization and find the Organizer's office. Its dome has dimmed with the fading light. I can see the full scope of it against the open sky, and the whole second story too, but the angle of the street and all the other buildings block off any view of the office's front doors. I risk a desperate lean off the roof but spot nothing.

"Shit," I say.

"Scout."

I almost die of a heart attack. I stick my head back into the ceiling opening to see Kieran and Pumpkin staring up at me. "What are you doing?" Kieran whispers. "Door's open."

I nod to him and turn to give the domed building a last hopeful look. Still, nothing moves. No noise echoes out. None that I can hear, anyway. I descend back inside and, as planned, let the descender pluck the anchor at the top. It's an easy grappling-hook shot to escape when we're done, and worth the extra time to keep our being here a secret.

"You see them?" Kieran asks on the way down, and I shake my head. "Well, whatever, you're going to like this at least."

This is a floor hatch beyond the now-open armored door. Kieran's already opened it too, or perhaps it was open before. I'm too excited to ask because there's a ladder leading down into a narrow, tunneled passageway. Motes of dust catch on the beams of our three headlights as we stare down. Above the hatch, engraved into the wall, is a map of the building's underground facility. It's a practical hive, all long tunnels and carved-out spaces in the earth.

"You're a genius," Kieran says.

"What? You're the genius."

"Well." He shrugs. "Let's both be geniuses."

Pumpkin meows because I'm pretty sure he believes he's the real genius out of the three of us.

14

Around a sloping bend, the tunnel floor levels out at last, and the steel walls give way to long panes of reinforced windows. Our headlights sweep over and through centuries of dust on the glass, illuminating the hollowed-out cavern beyond, the walls and windows of other rooms and floors this path might lead us through. Defunct technologies like lights, surveillance hubs, and communication systems line and dot the dry red earth of the cave walls, as still and silent as everything else.

Kieran jump-starts or shorts the old door tech with his decryption and override tools, gaining us entry to sparse rooms littered with ruined desks and benches, empty beakers, and shattered screens. One room houses a long table and a dozen toppled chairs, another just rows and rows of cots, thinner and longer than our own beds and so eroded and turned to dust that I can't learn much more. I poke at the refuse below bedsprings with my boot, wondering whether any of the eroded detritus was once a pillow or a blanket, maybe a gel pad or a sealant for a waterbed.

"Hey." Kieran walks right through to the other side of the long, rectangular room. Not everyone finds beds so fascinating. He's staring at the image he took of the map upstairs. "Cache still north?"

I pluck the tracker off my belt. It sure is. I nod at him.

He grins. "I think it's just down this hall."

Adrenaline bubbles up my chest into a long exhale. I rush to follow him into the next passageway, watching the tracker's bulky screen and the red dot upon it, blinking closer and closer. We reach a door, shut and locked like all the others, but I press my face to the hallway window and see that the room beyond has spherical walls and is coated in panes of glossy black material, a little like solar panels. Pumpkin sits beside Kieran, who's already hard at work on the door's thin locking mechanism, and meows. It's a tiny, sweet thing that means *Success!* Or maybe *Feed me.*

The electronic reader Kieran's tinkering with spurts with a celebratory spark like confetti, and with a scraping whine the door slides up and then jams halfway. It's enough to get a glimpse of the sleek black floor beyond, the reflection of some small, blinking source of light.

"Good enough," Kieran says.

I clap him on the shoulder. "More than good enough." I love my brother and his nerdy-ass, glorified lockpicker's skillset. And I'm beyond giddy at that blinking red dot, just meters away.

We crawl under the door after Pumpkin and push to a stand in a tiny, spherical room. The walls are lined in those same sleek panels I saw on its exterior, and a half-dozen bundles of wires lead from sockets between them to a central, cylindrical platform much like the one where we found the cache on Panev. On it, a short neon strip of light blinks slowly.

"Shit," I say. "We found it."

Kieran trots up to the platform, already pulling extraction tools out of his pack. "It's almost exactly the same."

"The room's a lot smaller."

"I mean the casing. The cache." He slides his pack to the floor and kneels so I lose sight of him behind the barrel-like storage core. Pumpkin disappears behind him, then comes around the other side, sniffing through his helmet along the floor. "You know," Kieran says.

He's stock-still with the uplink in his hand, waiting to do something. "If Verity Co. is still looking..."

The anticipation drains from me, leaving me cold enough with worry that I shudder. He's asking me for permission to do a rush job, and he's right to. The Verity grunts could be out there in all that dark behind us.

But they could also still be up top, drilling into the Organizer's office, right? Even if I didn't see or hear them from the top of the Sciences building, where else would they be? Maybe they'd just gotten deep enough inside that I wasn't able to spot them. And Archivist policy is strict. With good reason. Who knows what data might have been strained or corrupted when Verity Co. halted the copy on Panev, when they wrenched it from its housing without bothering to back it up?

"I feel like time might be of the essence here," Kieran says.

I want to squeeze my temples but can't, so settle for rapping my own helmet twice with my knuckles. "We have to."

There's a flicker of defiance in his face like he's about to disagree with me, but he relents, shaking his head. "Yeah, you're right." He starts the copy. "Looks like there's a greeting queued up in the emitter like last time. Casing is intact and the indicator light is on, so it should be safe."

"Play it," I say.

There's a soft fluttering sound. The glass bead on top of the cache burns with light and shoots out not one but several holographic Stelhari. They fill the room, moving to and fro with boxes or standing beside each other to compare charts and data. Pumpkin startles and scampers toward me for cover, little booties slipping without friction.

None of the Stelhari are Blyreena, which I should have expected but for some reason comes as a surprise. A single person approaches the forefront of the display, stepping toward me, toward the door. Based on what I remember from the *Hello World* documents, he's male. Slightly broader shoulders, a more intensely angular face, brightly colored, marbled skin. He wears a trite, tired sort of expression that pinches his eyes shut in a wince.

"This is Panev's head of Sciences, Nyaltor Vekterran. We have learned this day of the Endri's destruction of a number of planets: Clu, Sunyar, Darmar..." He lists several more, each name costing a heavy breath, but none so much as the last. "Panev," he says.

I draw breath with him. I should not be surprised that Panev fell. I should not be surprised that Blyreena surely was among those who perished. But there is a dissonance when he says it, when I think, *But she's here, she speaks to me on my ship.*

"The path the Endri takes across our systems will

lead it here, soon," Nyaltor says. "The information we've collated cannot be lost. I and the science team here have made contact with Galan in the Piori system. We've made arrangements to take our research there immediately."

I make a note of this in my suit's computer. There's more to find. Their story didn't end here. This world is destroyed, but maybe they found success on the next.

Pumpkin meows at me, and I shush him, refocusing on Nyaltor. "They've been studying Remnants there since the Endric collapse of Yerra-4 over a year ago," he says.

The Stelhari's name for Remnants is Endris Tinis—roughly, *tiny Endri.* My translator pops up the possible connection to Remnant, and I quietly confirm it.

"Hopefully, they have something more than what we've managed to come up with on our own, but, given our findings, given the speed of the Endri… ultimately, I suspect we will need to take our research to—to give our last stand on—"

Pumpkin hisses, but not at me. I yell out half of Kieran's name before something hard slams between my shoulder blades. I hit the ground so hard I bounce. Kieran cries out at our invisible assailants as a boot keeps me from rising. Another boot, steel-heeled and well aimed, crunches into my wrist as I reach for the flimsy little pistol at my belt. The pain whips up my whole arm like hot metal under the skin.

The clamor of our struggle stops, and Nyaltor's voice is cut unceremoniously short. The room returns to darkness as each Stelhari snuffs out. My pulse is a wave in my ears, accompanied by a worrisome ringing. Everything's still blurry from the bounce, but there's June above my brother near the cache, wrenching the uplink—the in-progress cache copy—from his hand. He relinquishes it at the threat of her nanobeam pistol, and she tosses it to the ground and fires upon it. It dissolves from the crater of her shot outward, turning to nothing.

I struggle, and the boot on my back presses its whole weight. I can't gasp out my angry rebuttal for a lack of breath, but inside I'm snarling. Pumpkin bats futilely at the boot on my wrist. He's shaking with rage, trying to bite through the glass of his helmet.

Above me, the man laughs, surprisingly delighted and soft despite my helmet's reflection of his gun aimed at my head. "Oh, look at him go."

I twist to escape but only manage to pop something in my back. "Headbutt him," I gasp, and Pumpkin rams the boot, causing the guy to become slightly hysterical.

"Oh wow, oh look, he's so cute."

"Gunner. Seriously?" June finishes wrenching the

cache from its housing with one hand, the other still holding the pistol aimed at my brother. "We're good."

She takes a few steps back from Kieran and the cored housing, and Gunner steps off me. I take my first full breath and roll over, pushing myself to sit. Pumpkin bops my elbow like he's expecting a treat.

"You two can leave now," June says behind me.

I turn to face her. "We know where they went, where the next cache might be."

"We heard it too."

"Just work with us," I snap. "We want the same thing here."

"We don't, though."

"Your Archivists aren't going to pay us," Gunner says. His guns and bandolier and exosuit all click as he shifts from foot to foot.

Kieran backs away slowly from June, whose gun is still loosely aimed in his direction, first in a crawl, then a crouch. He gets to me and scoops up Pumpkin, who asks *him* for a treat. "Let's go," he tells me.

"How did you find us?" I shout, ignoring him.

June nods to Gunner, who marches toward her. They're going to phase away like they did on Panev.

"We're just going to follow you," I say.

"Don't," Kieran warns.

"We're just going to keep going after the caches."

June smirks. "Bye, Scout."

"They're too valuable to give to fucking Verity Co.!" I call, but they're gone, phased back to their ship somewhere on the surface. "Fuck!"

"What is wrong with you?" Kieran is glaring at me. He shakes his head. "They could have killed us. They would have been in their right to kill us." He squeezes Pumpkin so tightly he squeaks.

"I had to—"

"No." My brother's face scrunches. He's angry. "You didn't. I don't want to die out here. I don't want you to die out here."

"We need to get back to the dinghy."

"We're not going to beat them there."

I close my eyes because I feel like yelling, but I don't want to yell.

"Scout," he says. "I don't think we can—"

"Please. I can't lose this."

Pumpkin meows. It echoes off the spherical walls, then settles into an absent silence once more. My pulse is thunder in my ears.

"Okay," Kieran says. He waits until I open my eyes and then nods at me. "Okay."

We duck under the jammed door and run toward the surface.

15

The sun has set. Our headlights bounce across the ruins of Nebul as we sprint toward our dinghy. I have never run this fast in my life. I'm panting for every smidgen of air my oxygen supply can give me, and when I reach the hatch, I'm so out of breath I have to hang over my knees and gulp three wheezing lungfuls before I can call out, "Kieran! Let's go!"

He reaches the hatch at last, and we dip inside. I'm repeating the planet and system Nyaltor mentioned over and over again in my mind as I strap Pumpkin in, then myself. Kieran goes to power the dinghy on, and I brace myself for the rumble of the engines.

But it doesn't come.

He dials the sequence to activate power again, pulls the lever. Nothing.

I inhale sharply into my burning throat and cough. "What's wrong?"

"I don't know." He goes through the sequence two more times, then unbuckles himself. Pumpkin meows, following Kieran with big eyes as he opens the hatch back outside.

"What's wrong?" I call again, because there's nothing else in my brain. Something is wrong. What is it? Why is it? I unbuckle myself and jog outside to find him. When I do, he's pushing aside an opened panel near the nuclear supply. I think, *Wow, he opened that fast*, and then I realize how impossible that is.

"Those fuckers!" I shout. I look to the sky, because they're out there somewhere, maybe looking down to see if their little sabotage worked. "Fuck you, June! Fuck you, Gunner! Fuck you, Verity Co.!"

"That'll help," Kieran says.

"Well," I snap. Well, what? He's right. He's always right. I pace in a small circle. "What did they do?"

"Severed the supply line to the engine."

My heart skips a beat and skids into a rough palpitation. "Is the nuclear core—"

"Energy's still there. They didn't kill us."

I sigh with relief. Nuclear power cores are nearly limitless supplies of energy for this and our main ship's needs. If Verity Co. had done something to drain it (or detonate it, as the movies would have you believe), we really would be dead. There's no food on this planet. No water. No realistic way to get back to orbit. I shudder to think about if these had been different people, and then I balk at my own ability to be *grateful* for them not murdering us.

"So we can fix it?" I say.

He pulls his head out of the dinghy's innards, already on it. "Yeah, but…" He wipes greasy hands on his suit and gives me a grim look. "It's going to take some time."

"How much time?"

"How long are this planet's days?"

"Twenty-eight-something standard hours."

He nods slowly. "Might be able to get it running come morning."

"Morning." I throw my hands up and let them slap back down to my sides. "If I help, can we speed it along?"

I wouldn't be *completely* dead in the water without my brother. I have enough basic training to read through the well-written manuals and perform well-ordered steps, but he shakes his head. "No. And it's safer as a solo job. I've got to set up radiation shielding and everything."

"Okay…"

"And you can't be on the dinghy when I open it up."

"So, take a walk with Pumpkin, then," I deadpan.

He shrugs like, *That's the way it's got to be*, and I nod. I don't fight him. I have no fight left. This is his specialty, and I have to trust he knows best. "Good luck," I tell him.

"I'll work as fast as I can," he mutters.

I duck back in the dinghy and free Pumpkin from his restraints. He yawns hugely, showing all his teeth, and curls right back into his seat. I couldn't sleep in this suit if you paid me, but cats are magic in any universe.

"Backpack it is," I say and rummage in storage for the cat pack. It's a hefty padded bag with a translucent dome bubble like a window, big enough for Pumpkin in his full gear, which means a big workout for me.

I get him inside with little resistance, and by the time I'm walking out of the dinghy, Kieran is already behind a radiation shield.

The city is silent under a sky filled with stars. I've been walking among the ruins for hours, poking around in offices that don't take too much hassle to get inside. The last thing my brother and I need is for me to get stuck somewhere and call for help.

I want him focused on getting the dinghy up and running. I want off this planet so we can get to the next one. I want to find Nyaltor's next cache. I want—I sigh—not to have let Verity Co. sneak up on us and steal *this* cache. I want a whole lot of things, and I'm not getting any of it.

I know it's clichéd, my dear, but all dark nights break to dawn.

It's our mom's voice in my head, strong and frail at the same time. Strong in conviction, frail in, well, actual physical strength. She's lying in a hospital bed, holding my hand, hooked up to about fifty different wires, a mask over her mouth so she can breathe easier. I'm on an alien planet millions of light-years from where she died, and I can still see her, still hear her voice.

Bad days beget bad memories, I guess.

I dig through my bag, moving carefully around Pumpkin's curled-up, sleeping form. I've been at it for hours, studying this world's architecture, taking soil samples, transcribing all the text on all the buildings. I've taken images, measured chair dimensions, discovered the ruins of some vehicle with smooth wheels and sundered electronics. I've done a lot in the time Kieran's been working, but I haven't used *that.*

I pull the VR overlay device from an armored pocket and clip it into the external drive receptor in the arm of my suit. Sometimes this makes my moods worse rather than better, but this is the next phase of my exploration, a necessary, different angle on everything I've viewed so far. I wait for the display to flash along the inside surface of my helmet on the heads-up display.

"Activate hindsight module," I say, and the thin holographic text begins churning out code and signs that it's processing. Sometimes I'll let the process run *off-screen*, as it were, so I can do other things without distraction in the interim. But today, now, I watch because I can't make Kieran work faster. I can't project myself hours ahead into a future where I can get to work translating the cache copy we have or finding the next planet. I can't go back to the past and post a guard at our dinghy, make myself stay back, so that Verity Co. doesn't mess with it. I have to be here. I have to do what I can here.

The thin pink text trailing past my vision moves too fast and choppy to fully understand, but I catch snippets, see the lines highlighting aspects of the terrain, sampling their aesthetic, hypothesizing about chemical compounds. *Iron saturation*, I catch. *Oxygen level. Distance to system sun. Humidity.*

I watch it focus and highlight the buildings, the sky, the concrete, the little patch of dirt where I planted the seeds. *Complete*, it flashes. *Overlay Hindsight Compilation?*

"Yes," I say, and my helmet fills with a new world.

Artificially computed, it fills out from me in a wave, holographic light running over everything, turning it all into what it might have been before all this. Before the destruction, the death, the ruins. Holes and fissures and cracks in buildings fill in, their doors are repaired, their windows unshatter. The streets are smoothed over. Rubble re-amasses into straight, flat lines. A fountain outside the financial office reconfigures and resumes its spewing, letting out torrents of crystal-clear water.

I walk along the road toward the Organizer's office. It is massive and beautiful, its dome top shining the gold of yesteryear instead of the decayed, sickly green we saw upon landing. As I walk, the overlay opens bubbles in the projection, showing me where modern-day rubble threatens to disrupt my steps. It juts out, cold and ugly, against this beautiful world that once was. So, I stop. I long to feel what breeze might have sucked through this grid of construction. I long to know what it might have smelled like, what temperature it was.

I look around for a long while and can't stop myself from thinking of Mom again. I involuntarily conjure an image of her, imagine what she would say if she were here, what things she would look at.

I look where she would look—at the sky—and think that maybe I can smell something new after all. Something clean and citrus-like. Warm blacktop being cooled. I imagine I am a Stelhari stepping out into the night for a break from all that work underground. I envision others walking the starlit roads. I put Blyreena on the steps of the Organizer's office, Nyaltor and his team of scientists around the fountain.

I try my hardest to imagine it, but all I see—all I *really* see—is nothing. All I really hear is my brother working on the dinghy. All I really smell is the sterile workings of my suit's filtration systems. That's all any of this is, because a millennium ago the Endri came and wiped out absolutely everything.

Did it know what it was doing, what it was taking away?

Did it care?

16

It feels like the longest day of our lives. When we're finally aboard the *Waning Crescent*, it takes everything not to pass out, everything not to just go to bed after the sanitation protocols finish, after we're out of our suits and Pumpkin's waddled off to the couches for rest. I've been saying the name of the planet Nyaltor mentioned over and over again for sixteen standard hours straight. It's so ingrained that when I go to our partial cache copy from Panev to retrieve the coordinates, I hardly have to think at all.

Either by luck or common decency, June and Gunner have not found a way to disable our ship. Maybe they couldn't find it, but we doubt that. Kieran puts the coordinates in, locks in the autopilot, and we're off through the stars. We don't say anything other than what we have to, to get things moving. I almost fall asleep in the copilot's chair, but somehow make it to my cabin.

It feels like I've slept the sleep of the dead. It's afternoon, my pillow is wet with drool, and it takes a solid ten seconds to even remember where I am. The first thing I can think of when I arrive wearily at the den, when I see Kieran equally dazed and bleary-eyed, rousing from his own sleep of the dead, is that I want a pizza.

"Yes, please," Kieran says, but he slumps against the couch, which means it's my turn to make it.

That feels exceedingly fair, given he fixed the dinghy to get us here. I even make his favorite: sausage, onion, and peppers, which I'm not super fond of. I think maybe he likes this flavor best because I pick off all the peppers and onions and give them to him. I do this in advance and pile all the vegetables on his side. My side gets hot sauce and a packet of artificial cheese dust.

Kieran is so tired that when I return, he hasn't put anything onscreen. "You alright?" I set the pizza on a tray between our seats.

He sits up and grabs a slice. "Mm," he grunts, like a half yes, half no. "Tired."

We eat in silence for a slice and half, which is weird. Pumpkin's not even around.

Ah, wait. His ears are *just* sticking out from the basket we threw our undersuits in to be washed. He likes his space, but he doesn't like to be far. I remember his attack on Gunner and smile, despite myself. I hate the guy, I really do. I'm hoping to everything their ship has malfunctioned in jump space, that they're waylaid and forced to make repairs. He's Verity Co.—the worst—but he thought my cat was cute.

"We have to be ready when we hit Galan." I wipe my hands on my lounge shorts and forgo the third slice, for now.

Kieran's considering his fourth. He shakes his head. "Okay. Well, we can't do anything about that now."

"We can talk about it. About how we're gonna handle things when we get there."

It's a short trip, roughly two standard days. Verity Co. isn't there yet. They can't be. Maybe they're slacking right now. Overconfident. Lazy. We can't beat them there but we can beat them with a plan.

Kieran sighs. "We don't know anything about where we're going. We don't know what the situation's going to be when we get there. Verity Co. could have already landed and left."

"Wow. Downer." I smile, but he doesn't.

"Just, put on a movie or something."

"What's your problem?"

He closes his eyes, frustrated—at me? at Verity

Co.?—and waves absently toward the projection table. I watch him there with his eyes closed for a few moments, but he doesn't say anything else. I flip through some options: something classic, something new, something quiet, something with a lot of explosions and robot fights.

Maybe he's mad at me. Maybe, if it weren't for me, we could have gotten Nebul's cache and gotten out before June and Gunner found us. I was the one who insisted he make a copy.

I stop scrolling through the database. "Kieran, what's on your mind?"

He groans, frustrated. I don't know why he's being so dodgy about whatever's going on. It's weird. He opens his eyes, grimaces, rolls his head back and forth like he's thinking through how to put things. At least he's gonna put them out there at all. I hate a stalemate.

"You could have gotten us killed yesterday," he says finally.

Reflexively I open my mouth to counter, but there's nothing to say. I scoff instead. *So what?*

"Seriously." He looks me in the eye, and he looks a little bit like Mom when she was lecturing us something good. "They have the tech to keep us at bay, but they had weapons too. Verity Co. is ruthless. They could have put us down. Me, you, Pumpkin. They would have been in their right to."

"They wouldn't have been *right* to," I snap.

"For Verity Co.? For interfering with"—he makes air quotes—"what's theirs?"

"What was I supposed to do? Let them take the cache without a fight?" He's working through a response, but I don't let him find it. "The Stelhari knew, Kieran. They knew. They studied what's wiping out all life in the universe."

"I know."

"Doesn't that mean anything to you? Isn't that worth fighting for?"

He closes his eyes to think, and I know I've got him on the run. "Of course it is. But—"

"But what?"

He sighs, shakes his head with something pretty clear in his eye: defeat. Surrender. But not to me. "If we've found what you think we've found, if these caches hold the answers to the Remnants and whatever spawned them, don't you think even Verity Co. will have to share that information? They're not going to let our worlds be destroyed."

Again I open my mouth, again nothing comes out. He's right. Maybe. Maybe he's right. But if we found the caches, if we brought this information back to the Archivists, I would never have to wonder. I could be certain that what we found was going to the right people. And maybe I want to be the one to deliver this universe-saving information so badly because I hate Verity Co. I really do. Everything they've done, the society they've created. Mom. Who would they save with any information found in this cluster? The people who could pay for it? The people who would sell their lives for it?

"Maybe," Kieran says, "we should go home."

It's like being slapped. "What?"

"It's Verity Co." He looks down at his lap. "They're two for two, and now they have another head start. Even if there's a hundred other caches in this cluster, they kind of, well, they kind of have us beat." He gives me a grim, apologetic look. "I know this is important to you—"

"To me?" I laugh, angry and helpless. "But not to you?"

"Of course to me, but…" He swings his hands up and lets them fall. *What can we do?*

What can we do, indeed. Verity Co. is impenetrable. Insurmountable. They have the tech. They have the head start. They've retrieved the complete caches from Panev and Nebul, assuming they weren't damaged by the hasty extractions. Even if we get the next one, will it be enough? Won't Verity Co. just get back to their headquarters and patent any relevant information before we can even start to break it down? Why not go home? Why not give up?

I've failed. I keep doing this, keep failing. Why doesn't anything I do amount to anything?

"I'm gonna go." I stand up. "Stay on standby. Maybe we change course for home, maybe we..."

"Scout," Kieran says, like he wants to keep talking, but I press ahead until I can't hear whatever else he's trying to say.

17

I hate it, but Kieran's right. I try to think through some ways we might beat Verity Co. to the next cache, things we can do to outmaneuver them, their own lack of cultural understanding we can exploit, but without knowing anything about Galan except its coordinates and pre-annihilation population (roughly two million), there's nothing I can plan for that would actually make a difference. There's nothing I can do.

It makes me wonder if there's anything I could do even if I had the caches. Even if I went back to the Archivists, would the information be useful? Could we decipher it in time? Our civilization is surrounded by a graveyard, but it's like only the Archivists understand what that means, what that portends. I think about how hard the Stelhari tried, about the caches they left behind. I think about how all the worlds we've been to have been dead anyway.

I think about Mom. I think about tomorrow. I think about how she's dead anyway.

I sigh and sit at my desk.

Blyreena, give me something. Please.

Recording Playback 1.0023.498.x

Speaker and Authorizer: Organizer President, Interstel Councilmember Sy. Blyreena Ekstafor

Rotation 2, Mayak Harvest, 3550

Each day I sat unemployed—not a student, not a worker, not anything—I thought back to that review I was given for my thesis. It's so easy, when things don't go as we planned, to think that we're a failure. To think that things will never get better. In those long days I sat applying to doomed endeavors, I had something like a crisis of faith. Was everything I'd worked for doomed to failure? What was I without my dream?

It says a lot of Ovlan that despite my deteriorating mood, we moved in together about a month after graduating, around when his new job began. We rented an apartment together near the Sciences Spire, and again, despite everything, were getting along well. He had this miraculous ability to turn even the worst of my moments into positive ones, into something funny or, at the very least, something worth learning something from. There was always the fear that once we'd graduated and lost the student status that had allowed us to bond, we would fall apart. But we didn't.

In the first few weeks of his job, in between when he was training and meeting people and becoming comfortable with the administrivia, we spent much of our time putting our home together: acquiring furniture, setting up payments, stocking essentials like cookware and televisions and other such things we hadn't needed to worry about in the communal dormitories of the Academy. I found these necessary outings and chores mundane and bothersome in light of my incessant need for a job of my own.

I remember a particularly hard day. We had gone to a furniture outlet where we'd placed an order for a bed. This was a very important thing to get because we'd been sleeping on the floor and were having a hard time of it. The bed wasn't due for another several hours after we got there, as there had been a printing delay. I was so tired from a lack of sleep, and frustrated. We'd been spending money something close to lavishly, and despite my anxieties (and lack of income), Ovlan suggested lunch. On him, he joked. It was funny because, to my wounded pride, everything was on him.

We went to a little café on the lake. It was gorgeous. Sunny, cool. The spire glittered silver, and the summertime birds had arrived at last. The food was delicious.

I spent the entire time complaining about my job prospects, about the printing delay, about how we had to reschedule the movers, about how sore I was, how tired I was, how miserable I was, how maybe, that reviewer had been right. It was Ovlan who pointed out the sun, the coolness, the birds, how amazing the food was.

I think I told him he was being insensitive. He told me it was a beautiful day.

I was mad at him after that, even when we arrived at the furniture outlet a few hours later to pick up the bed. We arrived right behind the movers we'd hired to transport it to our apartment, and we, they, and the printing technicians gathered as the thing was arriving hot off the press. I wanted to be anywhere else; I wanted to be home, applying for jobs. In the last stages of dismounting from the printing platter, the bed slipped. It crashed several meters to the floor and cracked, right down the middle. Both printing technicians put their hands over their mouths with shock, and me, well, I burst out laughing. And crying. But mostly laughing. And the technicians laughed, and Ovlan laughed, and the movers laughed.

I was stressed maybe, or perhaps it was a nervous breakdown. But it had felt good to laugh. I laughed all the way home after arranging for a new bed and another day for the movers. When Ovlan and I collapsed onto our makeshift bed at home—blankets and pillows and carpeted floors—I was still laughing.

"See," he told me. "Beautiful day."

On that, at the time, I disagreed. It was an awful day, I told him, but I do think I apologized for being morose about the whole thing.

Now, it's funny. Now, I can *really* laugh about it. Now, I can see that he was right: that it had been a beautiful day. A memorable day, at the very least, and one of the last where Ovlan and I had so much free time to do what we needed and wanted. It's strange what hindsight does. Takes all the layers of emotions and flattens them, turns them either good or bad. It can take time to see the shadows as something beautiful.

But of course, in the present, hindsight is not possible. The present is messy, scary, uncertain. There was so much good in those weeks when Ovlan was just beginning his career. But living through it at the time, I saw no way to the other side, no bridge between me and my own job, my own opportunity to leave my mark on the world.

Things became harder when Ovlan's work finally began requiring him to travel to one of Panev's industrialized moons, Ilvi 10. He could hardly contain his excitement for the work: expanding living communities for researchers and their families, including a localized terraforming project similar to what had given his hometown healthy crops so many years before. His trips to Ilvi 10 ranged from several days to several weeks, and though I was proud of him—so proud of him—it was a pride difficult to reconcile with my own feelings of failure.

I wish I could say I was always supportive. I wish I could say I never let my failings and doubts turn to jealousy, or my jealousy to coldness. He would remind me, years later, that I was only Stelhari, that I had weaknesses, feelings, that I could not have been expected to be perfect, but...

When he came home, he would ask, *What have you done?* And I would assume he really meant, *Why have you done nothing?* He would say, *Something will come around.* And I would hear, *You're a failure for nothing having come yet.*

Had that reviewer been right? I constantly wondered. Had they been such a force in the field and hated my work so strongly that they put me on some invisible blacklist of people never to hire?

I was applying for jobs within the Organizers at every opportunity: science liaison positions, economics liaisons. Even secretarial jobs, the sorts of things I had completed for internships between semesters. I wanted anything at all. I had worked so hard. I had done everything right. Good grades, an advanced degree, internships, volunteer work—everything. There was no deeper feeling of failure than to complete all the prerequisites for happiness and yet not achieve it.

Ovlan was on one of his lengthier work trips, months into his job, when I finally received an invitation for an interview at the head Organizer's office. I could hardly believe it. It was a breath of fresh air. A hand to hold in the dark. Refuge from the feeling of drowning. It was like being resuscitated, that invitation, like being granted permission to feel joy again.

I called Ovlan right away, and he talked me through everything. We practiced interview questions face-to-face through the screen. He ran me through worst-case scenarios, best-case scenarios. He stayed up with me every night for a week, and on the night before the interview, sat with me for hours practicing, belaying my fears. I kept saying, *Go to bed,* and he kept saying, *You first.*

We ended the night watching an episode of *Food Truckers Across the Stars.* I don't remember the whole thing, only waking up to my alarm come morning. Ovlan was no longer on his side of the video feed, but it hadn't stopped. He'd left a note there, positioned to face the camera. *I love you,* it said. *Good luck.*

That night, after the interview, he stayed up with me again. And again for the second round of interviews, a week later. He'd put on a little party ribbon and had somehow managed to get his hands on fizz. We got high a million kilometers away from each other and watched movies. I would find out the next day if I got the job, so we watched the best food comedies Panev had to offer. We went to bed late into the night. I woke in the early afternoon, and again he'd left a message in place of himself: *I love you. I'll see you tonight.*

By that time of day, Ovlan was already on the shuttle back to Panev. I did what I could for my nerves solo. I walked around the lake in the shadow of the Sciences Spire. I stopped at the café we'd gone to together that terrible, beautiful day with the bed. I checked every notification tentatively, as if the alert might bite me. I was walking home under the setting sun when I got the call.

I waited until the last possible ring to answer, and when I did—

When I did, it was an offer.

I practically sprinted the rest of the way home,

where I collapsed on the couch from sheer joy. I had done it. I had gotten the job. Nearly six months after graduating with an advanced degree and something had finally come through. I cried with relief. I danced. I scoured the net, prepared for my shopping spree for professional attire. I sent a quick message to Ovlan—*I got it!*—and ordered our favorite food for delivery. A celebration for my job; a celebration for him coming home.

I watched the door, too excited to do anything else in the fifteen-minute window he usually arrived in. But he didn't arrive.

I kept watching that door. He'd been due for over an hour. The food had come. I'd needed to put it in the cooler so it wouldn't spoil and congeal. I sent him a message: *Are you okay?* Half an hour later I sent him another. Half an hour after that, I began to pace.

There is a certain amount of terror that won't let one sit still. My messages became more frequent, more frenetic. A gut feeling took over, so repulsive that I could not stand it. I offered up my job if he came home safe—a cosmic, karmic trade. I offered up my designer bed and my favorite shows and my favorite food and anything.

There was a knock on our apartment door two hours after he was due home. I tugged it open.

Ovlan stood there, drenched from the rain, a

package under one arm, the handle of his suitcase in another. "Sorry," he said. "I couldn't open the door myself, with all this."

I threw my arms around him and did not let him go. "You beast!" I lectured him terribly. "You had me scared half to death!"

"My personal broke," he explained, fighting my arms to slip out of his wet clothes. "I dropped it on the shuttle and that was that."

"But you're so late!" I was rather whiny, but I felt I'd earned it. I thought maybe I owed it to the universe to give up all the things I'd said I would. I didn't regret the bargains. If I could no longer taste roast eveck or if *Food Truckers* got canceled, so be it.

"I was getting you something." Ovlan gestured to the thin, square package he'd brought.

"What for?"

He smiled, and at his encouraging nod, I opened the package. It was a framed holotext, written in neon-blue lines with a faded cream background. The whole thing looked rather professional. It was a quote, and one I was devastatingly familiar with: the concluding remarks of that reviewer who had smeared my work and spirit so terribly.

"I thought it would be a nice thing to hang in your new office," Ovlan said with the cheekiest grin you can possibly imagine. "Right next to your advanced degree and official Organizer's nameplate."

I laughed so hard I cried. Or maybe I laughed hard and cried hard, each of their own accord. I could not have asked for a better partner, a better lover or friend. No one is owed an Ovlan, but I was so lucky.

We chatted for hours, ate dinner, turned on a show in the background. We talked about my new job, his job, how things were going. We talked about planning a trip to see his parents, or mine. When the energy of our reunion simmered down, when the breaks between our voices became longer, something dawned on me. "How did you know?" I asked. "Your personal is broken. How did you know I got the job?"

He shrugged. "I just knew."

"If you had been wrong, it would have been the most terrible gift imaginable."

He laughed, my Ovlan. "Hadn't even thought of that," he said and kissed me.

I couldn't believe my luck. Him. My job. In that moment, that I had been unemployed and miserable for months seemed a sort of bad dream. Finally, some of Ovlan's good humor and nature was rubbing off on me. It's hard to tell in the moment, but with hindsight I can see that when I keep pushing forward, things have a way of working out.

★ ★ ★

I pause the recording. Blyreena stands frozen, tall and smiling, iridescent eyes warm despite all the coolness in their color.

I haven't gotten anything about the Endri from her. I haven't heard anything at all about the crisis that befell her worlds, or the defenses her people were mounting against it. But in this moment, for the first time, I don't really care. I'm listening to her. I'm hearing her.

"Kieran," I say. I've called him through our intracomm. "I'm sorry. We can't go home just yet."

18

I know what day it is when I wake up, because my chest is heavy. And sure, I know the date on the calendar, so I knew it was coming, but there's a feeling that comes with waking up on the day, like part of me has turned to stone. There's a smell in the air too, an impossible one, but it's so real I can't deny that somehow Kieran smuggled aboard the supplies to make Mom's favorite dish. I sigh at the cloying tropical-fruit stench, the warm allure of baking pastry. The memory of our last meaningful time together hits like lightning, and I swing my legs out of bed so fast it's sure I've been hit by some. Pumpkin jumps off me, ruffled with surprise.

"Sorry," I tell him, and the word comes out raw. I press my fingers to my eyes and rub out the burning behind them. "Breakfast?"

He's placated by the offering and settles back down to clean himself while I dress. Binder, tank, trunks. Everything picked right up off the floor where I tossed it all the night before. The fruity scent hits harder when I open the door. I pause in the frame for a moment. I'm half mad at Kieran, half too sad to care.

He's not in the den when Pumpkin and I pass by, and though the kitchen bears the brunt of the smell (and the mess), he's not there either. I get Pumpkin his morning allotment of crunchies and wander until I find my brother in the cockpit. He's got a baking tray of yellow pastries on the copilot's chair and one pastry half-eaten in his hand.

"Hey," he says and moves the tray into his lap. I sit. "Want one?"

"Didn't see any of this in food storage." We went over inventory together with an Archivist operations lead before leaving home. Nothing gets aboard a ship without close scrutiny, unless…

"I knew you wouldn't agree to it, so I used personal storage."

"Why?"

"Because Mom would've wanted one." He thrusts the tray at me. "And they're delicious. Stop looking at me like I punched you, and take a damn pastry."

I take a damn pastry.

Mom came home from an Archivist operation in

the Bolvin Cluster about two years ago, wanting to go "somewhere the complete opposite of frigid wasteland." We went to an artificial island resort near the equator, reclaimed and reconstructed into the glorious swath of sunny beaches it had been before climate change sank most of home's islands right into the sea.

It was a Verity Co. installation, of course. But Mom didn't care. I hadn't learned to care. We swam in temperature-controlled oceans, stayed in lavish, temperature-controlled beach huts, and ate lab-grown fish and crustaceans whose DNA donors had once roamed the dead waters the worlds' richest organization had revived back to life for tourists. Mom didn't care for seafood, turned out.

But this one little shop we went to along the beach... she saw the pastries in the window and smelled the smell and ducked right in and bought three. Later she bought a dozen, to our knowledge, and about ten dozen—not to our knowledge—but that was another memory. Pumpkin followed her dutifully for every trip. Her favorite child, Kieran and I liked to joke.

The owner of the shop descended directly from the peoples who used to live on the islands before they sank and were built up anew with rebar and steel. The recipe was old, and Mom fell in love with it. She said it was the realest thing at the whole resort.

"Do you remember," Kieran says, smiling, "when

customs opened that bag at the port, when we were leaving?"

And there it is. I laugh weakly, despite my mood. Mom had ditched some clothes and replaced them with these pastries—not boxed pastries but just pastries, like she'd gone into the bakery and stolen about ten trays. She hadn't. She'd bought them. The luggage was so packed that when the port official finally popped it open, the things exploded out, like a prize. Everyone in the security line looked at us like we were crazy.

Kieran finishes laughing. "That was so embarrassing."

"And gross," I relent. I can't help smiling. I can feel my mouth stretch, take unnatural shape around the sadness. "Who the hell packs food like that?"

"Wasn't even wrapped."

"She was wild," I say, and sigh. The *was* always gets me.

"She went for what she wanted." Kieran frowns a little, then smiles at me, and I'm the first to break eye contact.

The window is full of light, like a wave that never breaks.

He finishes his pastry and wipes his hands on his pants, then places the tray on the dashboard, away from some of the more critical buttons. It's still not a good place to put it. "Not as good as the ones on the island," he says.

"No." I finish mine too. "But a good effort."

"For Mom," he says.

"For Mom," I say.

"Meow meow," Pumpkin says. He's arrived from the kitchen for pets.

I can't believe it's been a year. Sometimes it doesn't feel real, like when we go back home, she'll be there waiting for us. Sometimes, like right now, the memories hit so hard that I fall into them, and coming back to reality is like waking up from a dream too good to leave behind. I see blue skies and gold sandbars and her across a flimsy white plastic table, and then: me and Kieran, in the cockpit of the *Crescent*. I'll never get to share this breakfast with my mom again.

What kind of a universe is that, where islands are brought back to life, but people aren't?

Recording Playback 1.0023.498.x

Speaker and Authorizer: Organizer President, Interstel Councilmember Sy. Blyreena Ekstafor

Rotation 2, Mayak Harvest, 3550

Our wedding was less than a year after I got my position with the Organizers. We didn't make the largest deal of the event itself, or of the proposal. We were both busy with our jobs and wanted something small and intimate. The proposal wasn't even a surprise. We'd talked about marriage extensively, what we wanted, what we didn't want.

"Bly," Ovlan said on a night with rain. We'd planned that at least, the rain. A touch of romance never killed anyone. "If I didn't mind getting soaking wet, I'd take you outside, but I'm really cozy and kind of just want to sit here with you."

I laughed and turned toward him, overly proper and expectant.

"That said," he went on. We'd said no bond bracelets, so when he peeled open his hands to reveal something, I was surprised, a little scandalized really. But what rested between his palms was a poorly made, now sweat-soggy cookie with Sul Bnd? written on it in icing, because *Will you enter a soul bond with me?* could not have possibly fit.

I only let him sweat a moment.

At our wedding, I told the less than twenty attendees about the moment I knew for certain he was the one, which was when I learned he was afraid of snakes in his apartment two weeks after he sat with me while my transport was being repaired after its run-in with his. Ovlan told everyone he knew I was the one the moment I railed his new transport. We got a lot of laughs.

That night, we sat in the shade of a tree that had been on his family's land for hundreds of years. It was spring when we married, and its drooping, wave-like branches were flowering with pale blue blooms that smelled like salt and perfume. To just sit under its boughs was to feel history, to look across the plains and emptiness, to see what Ovlan's ancestors might have seen—sans the crop regulators. The sky was filled with stars like I'd never seen in the city. We spotted Ilvi 10. He waved, jokingly, to his boss way up there.

I rested my head against his in the quiet, in the ambient chirp of bugs and night fowl, in the low, persistent hum of the regulator nearby. The long grass edging from his parents' home to just before the rows of crops swayed like an ocean, caught the silvery shine of our moons and the universe. There was a breeze, soft and cold, that caressed when it blew by. Ovlan's hand was in mine, warm instead.

I told him, "This is the best moment of my life."

He squeezed my hand, shifted so that we sat face-to-face. He pressed his forehead to mine. The breeze sucked between our bodies, like wind through a canyon. The grass tinkled along with the birds. When he spoke, his voice resonated through me, through our skulls touching under the soft layers of our skin. "No," he told me, "this one is."

I tried to pull back, confused, but he held me

steady, kept our foreheads together, our hands together. I could just see his smile. "Now this one is," he said.

I could feel his fingers tracing circles in my palm, the soft tug of another breeze against my clothes. I could feel the ancient bench beneath me, smell the salt of the flowers, see the light of all those stars against all that land. I could feel his head against mine. I could feel my love for him like a lightening in my chest, like the flutter of a small, gentle creature.

"This one is," he said again, and later again, and again. That night, and many nights after, and standing in line at the grocer, doing dishes, or sitting on the couch watching our favorite show. In good times and bad; when we were happy or when we argued; when we read good news or ill, he would find the time to take my hand and whisper, "This one is."

19

The dinghy descends through the atmosphere like a butter knife through raw steak: roughly. Galan has turned out to be a rare dead world whose electromagnetic activity remained brutally in flux after its collapse. It's covered in violent, dry electrical storms, and that's about all I know beyond knowing I have a healthy fear of them. Our little boat rattles like a dysfunctional nuclear generator as we break through the clouds at last.

Below is a mountain range, all spindly, twisting, and tall. In the dark, their precipices look more like reaching tentacles than anything earthen, their shadows distorted and overlong with every flash of lightning.

Kieran takes manual control of the dinghy as the worst of the shaking subsides, steering us toward the coordinates for the cache we identified from orbit. It's still here. June and Gunner have likely beaten us here, but they haven't escaped with the prize. I hold on to that for hope as we rattle against a heavy blow of wind.

"Meow!" Pumpkin complains, and I completely agree.

"Can we go a little faster?" I squeak.

"Not without serious risk of death!" Kieran is gritting his teeth, but I know secretly he loves this stuff. Back home, there's a theme park with all these crazy rides. It's kind of kiddy in theme, but the roller coasters test the mettle of any adult. I can't ride them. Kieran rides them right after lunch and keeps it all in.

There's only one real place to land in the jagged mountain range, and it's by design. At a glance, this place looks like uncivilized wilderness. There's not a mortal-made structure in sight. But the cache is deep in the mountains, underground, just like on Nebul. So unless Verity Co. grabbed the goods from a city and ran to the wild for a vacation, the mountains actually conceal something intentionally built. Something important.

There are little ridges and outcroppings all over the mountain range, but there is exactly one tabletop cliff, flattened, smoothed out, and covered in some kind of poly-metal material obviously meant for the landing of small vessels like ours. It has markings that are all but entirely faded. Kieran brings the dinghy above the landing zone and begins to lower down.

BREEP-BEEP!

The proximity alarm is appropriately chilling and causes all three of us to gasp (or hiss). I hold my breath as Kieran frantically readjusts.

"Come on," I whisper. I want off the ride.

"But there was nothing there," he says, and moves laterally until the alarm stops. He doubles the thruster strength from last time, moving down minutely. No alarm blares. I look out the window as we touch ground—sweet, blessed ground!—and see he's right. There's nothing at a glance but—I tilt my head and catch the faintest mirage-like sheen—there *is* something there.

"They're definitely here," I say.

"You see something?"

"It's their ship, I think."

He unbuckles himself and leans over me to get a better view of where we almost crashed. "It *is* an ECOE. Never seen this kind of thing up close."

He sounds fascinated, but we're in a race against the quickest, sharpest, richest organization in the known living universe. "Kieran."

"Sorry." He pulls back and jogs to Pumpkin to undo his restraints.

"What's an echo, anyway?"

"Environmental concealment overlay emitter," he says. Pumpkin hops to the floor and joins me at the hatch. "Come on, that one's basic."

"Basic for a nerd." He scoffs as I open the way outside. The storm sounds worse now that we're exposed to it, like steel being ripped apart in a sealed chamber.

"Should we check it out?" he asks, and at my look clarifies, "The invisible ship."

Before I can suggest that maybe we should leave it alone, the staticky hiss of an external radio cuts through the rumble of the storm. A calm, feminine voice, cut to chops, says, "Captain June, First Officer Gunner, please respond." It repeats a few times, which is the only reason I can fully make out what it's saying.

I approach the sound and touch the surface of the nearly imperceptible vehicle to make sure it's really there, that the transmission isn't a figment of my imagination, or a ghost, or some strange effect of the electrical storm.

"Maybe we should answer it," Kieran says, sounding worried.

"I wouldn't know how to," I say.

He frowns and shakes his head. "Me either. We'd have to be able to deactivate the emitter somehow."

I look around. There's one entrance to the mountain's interior, a sentient-carved cave with a steel door leading into the dark. It's already open. The panel to its right is busted, and some thin metal buttons are scattered in the dirt, clattering around with the wind. I unclip the tracker from my belt. The cache is in there, somewhere.

I don't like this. I didn't even know Verity Co. was traveling with a third member. Maybe a fourth or fifth too. Who knows how many grunts there are? And is the problem this person is calling about up there? Or down here?

"Let's just do what we came here to do," I say. It comes out uneasy, but Kieran and Pumpkin follow after me anyway.

We pass through the opening and activate our lights, flooding the metal hallways with motes of dirt and dust. The construction is much less ornate than the underground structures of Nebul. There are no glass panels showing the mountain core beyond, or intricately stenciled maps at each turn showing the myriad but simple paths ahead.

We're stuck in just one hallway, leading one direction, our boots rapping softly off the steel. Far behind remains the half-oval portal to the outside, bright with lightning. A draft pulls in from it, a long, almost-mournful sucking toward somewhere up ahead. It whips dirt around our ankles, and Pumpkin shivers each time.

The rigid metal walls finally allow us to turn left, and—

"Whoa!" Kieran cries, and it echoes and echoes and

echoes, because right around the bend, he catches himself before falling forward into a massive cavern.

I pull him back from the ledge by his backpack, fingers clenched so tight around the strap that they ache. "Damn it, be careful."

"My bad," he says, like he ate a slice of my pizza instead of almost dying.

Pumpkin stops at the edge and sniffs. His headlamp and ours reveal the twenty-meter drop my brother almost took, right onto the steel surface of another tunnel below. It looks like a train car, almost. The top of it has been sawed open, probably by a plasma cutter, because the opening is a nearly perfect circle.

"Who do you think did this?" Kieran's moving his light over the jagged edges of the hall we're standing in and at the rest of the hall directly across from us, where we could have walked if it weren't for the enormous, tattered gap. Just inside it is a closed steel door, bulging out from the inside. A single thin fissure cracks its misshapen, protruding middle like a dark strike of lightning.

"I don't know," I say. I trace the tunnel exterior below and find pieces of thick, wiry metal at the bottom of the cavern, the same steel as the hall we're standing in. It all looks like shrapnel.

I check the tracker again, fidgeting with the holographic dials. The electrical storm and our journey into the mountain are wreaking havoc with the electronics, but I get the red dot that marks the cache to appear. It's moving steadily along the grid map, twenty meters down, almost eight hundred meters west, by estimation. It's moving fast.

"Looks like they have it," Kieran says, looking over my shoulder. Pumpkin lets out a low, mournful growl. His tail flicks, sitting there at the edge of the chasm. "Down we go?"

"I don't like this." I have to say it. My stomach hurts. That's as clear a gut feeling as things get.

But my brother smiles his usual reassuring smile. "It's moving because Verity Co. has it. And it looks like they're coming this way. We can intercept them and…"

It all stops there. What *do* we do if we run into Verity Co.? How will we stop them from taking the cache? We didn't get here first this time. We don't have a smidgen of a copy, a second of an emitted message. If we don't get *something* here, our journey may as well be done. We'll never find randomly what Verity Co. will with a map.

Kieran sees me coming up short and nods. "First step is getting to them. Let's start with that."

I put the tracker back to my belt and look over the chasm. "Okay." But gods, spirits, whoever—is that drop deep.

"You and Pumpkin go down first, okay?" He pulls

out the anchor and descender and starts unfurling the cord he's brought with him.

Pumpkin doesn't like getting in the chest harness, but he never does. I descend slowly, all the way through the circle cut in the roof of the tunnel like it was made for this very descent. I wonder if June and Gunner made this. I wonder if they cut through the hall up there or caused that splinter in that door.

I unbuckle Pumpkin at the bottom and manage to calm his feistiness a little in the time it takes Kieran to descend. Pumpkin's tail is flicking, and he has meowed a few more times, agitated.

"You okay, buddy?" Kieran gives him a little massage through his suit, but the little gourd stays on all fours. He's staring at the walls—same as the hall above, so far as I can tell—with scrutinizing intensity. I want to find Verity Co. and get out of here yesterday.

"Cache is this way." I point west and am already moving. Kieran falls into step behind me.

We walk a dozen paces, and there's a shift, the scrape of whining metal, like a damaged seafarer careening on a stormy sea, like a meteor rig bending in cosmic wind. It comes from up ahead, faraway and too close all at once.

"Come on." Kieran pushes past me and keeps walking. "It's just settling."

I'm frozen. But he starts to move past what my light

can see clearly, and I jog to catch up. Pumpkin's at my heels. He's no longer meowing. I catch up to my brother in time to turn the bend with him, and a short five meters away is another door, bulging out and cracked down the middle just like the one we saw in the hall above. Except the fissure is wider in this one. Big enough to stick even a helmeted head through. It dawns on me: something behind these doors was trying to break *out*.

"No." I grab Kieran.

"No?"

I don't know what to say. We need that cache. Our worlds need that cache. But I don't like this. The metal whines again, and this time it's closer. It's all around us. There's the slightest rumble under our feet, and Pumpkin begins to growl.

"Whoa." Kieran takes a step back from the door.

Another sound joins the metal whine, faint at first, but approaching rapidly: the unmistakable echo of gunfire—voices—footsteps. Me, Kieran, and Pumpkin, all three of us buckle. We're not trained for combat. We're not accustomed to the sounds of war or fighting—whatever it is. I'm scared out of my mind, and by the time my systems reboot, the noise is right on the other side of that busted door.

"Run!" I cry, and me and Pumpkin turn to book it. But Kieran doesn't.

He's rigid, watching as a figure tries to push through and gets stuck in the fissure in the door. It's June. She tries to part the metal with her hands, then sees us. "Please!" she yells over the yawning, terrible sound behind her. "Help us!"

20

My brother rushes to the ruined door and June. I rush to Pumpkin. He's puffed up and terrified, eyes as big as moons, and at a snap of gunfire, he turns tail to run. I pounce on him before he can get too far. He hisses and yowls as our bodies flatten to the floor. I pin his scrambling form in my arms and squeeze like if he gets away, I'll lose him. And I will, if he does. He bats me with his booties, and my stupid, shaking hands grasp numbly at the straps across my chest to bind him.

There's a flash of light behind the door, behind my brother and June, stuck halfway through. There's the *whumpf* of a sonic rocket, maybe, and Gunner's voice, maybe. He's shouting for June to *go*, to *hurry. It's coming.*

Pumpkin makes a desperate lunge, and I forgo fumbling with the straps for a better hold. I catch him by the hips, but he's slipping, slipping—

Metal rips apart. Kieran's shorted the card reader or lock or whatever it is in the frame, and the door pulls open a little more, highlighted by a flash from another rocket. It fires off from behind the door, bright as a flare, and through the slight crack in the door, I see it tail off into—into nothing. A mass of shiny black glitters in the light of the rocket like oil on water, like stars in the abyss, and then the rocket is swallowed. Not just the object, not just the light, but the *sound*. The screaming trajectory of the projectile is cut like a plug being pulled, and the darkness seethes closer.

Remnant. It's a Remnant.

"Kieran!" I scream. I want to run to him, drag him back from the door. It's not that I want June or Gunner to die. But courage has dropped out. Chivalry is dead. Terror is everything now, every moral, every ability to think. It's just: *Remnant, Remnant, Remnant.*

I squeeze Pumpkin to me with all the strength of one arm, and with the other pull just one of the straps all the way around him. It's not enough. He could slip or escape, but my whole body is shaking and Kieran isn't moving fast enough and there's a Remnant. A Remnant. I yell at my brother again.

He's shaking too, from head to boots, as he clutches June's flailing hands and pulls her through to our side. In her absence my light catches a swirl of dark and glimmering orbs like eyes. An icy draft, cold as death, snakes through the gap.

Gunner ducks down, squeezes partly through. June goes for him, but he's pulled backward—there and then gone—with a scream. It's earsplitting. Pained. Afraid. And then it's gone.

June cries out his name like all is lost. Something inside me wilts, hearing it.

But then she screams "*Go!*" and she and Kieran run right at me. Dark slips through the door like a tendril, like ink in water, and I'm snapped back to the need for my legs, to Pumpkin writhing against me, to my heart's frenetic sputter, to the fact, the idea, that we're next.

I turn and run. My knees buckle, but I catch myself. Pumpkin swings dangerously in the single strap, but I catch him. I'm the first to the cord and descender hanging through the hole in the ceiling. I reach for it, but it takes two tries for my shaking hand to grasp it. I fumble with the carabiner. My fingers have gone numb, it's so cold. Pumpkin howls.

I'm sorry, Pumpkin. I'm sorry.

"No time!" June catches up to me and tugs me along by the arm. She forces me into a full-paced sprint, then lets me go, leading the way. Kieran's right behind me.

I am not keen on trusting a Verity Co. grunt with my life, and my cat's life, and Kieran's life. But June is combat-trained, no doubt. June is not sobbing on the ground over Gunner's death. She is moving fast and leading the way through a labyrinth of hallways so assuredly that I'm certain she's moved through these spaces before. So I follow. I have no choice but to follow.

"Here!" she calls. We've reached a room that looks like it barely survived an explosion. Earthen rubble on the far side lets in cracks of light. The steel wall that once kept the earth and elements at bay has been sundered inward as if something once broke into this place, straight through the rock and steel, with one deadly, piercing motion.

Before I can stutter out a terrified suggestion, her grav shock boots jump her over two tables toward the rubble, and she plants a small device between the rocks. It detonates outward in a flash. Light pours in. The ground shakes. The cold hits my back in a wave like a draft, knocking me forward.

"Hurry!" June plants herself at the edge of the open wall and holds out her hand.

Kieran squeaks out a question, but he's running forward anyway. He grabs her hand, and she slingshots him—throws him—out the hole and to the right. He disappears.

I don't have time to freeze or doubt or worry or

question. I grab June's hand too, stumbling only a little at the relentless shaking. She flings me and Pumpkin.

For a moment, I am airborne in a mountain range. I thank Verity Co. despite it. I thank their tech and their exosuits and their gravity-adapting strength enhancers. I go flying two meters and land on a small outcropping about as wide. Kieran presses himself to the wall to dodge me.

When I land, catching myself so Pumpkin, swinging in his one strap, doesn't flatten beneath me, the ground is still trembling violently. Red dust is coming down like a waterfall. Behind me, rocks tumble and crack down the steep mountainside into the barely visible open mouth of the exploded cave we've left behind. Then there's June. She jumps the odd angle without the slingshot or any help, and dust and rocks rain over her. She's dropping too fast through midair, and I can't think, but something registers in my gut: she's not going to make it.

For a moment, I am airborne in a mountain range.

One of my hands closes over her forearm, hers over mine. My other snags our little ridge's edge, and together June's, my, and Pumpkin's weight all pop against those fingers. The arm bearing June pops too. Something dislocates. My grip on her goes slack; my fingers go numb. I think I can still feel her holding on to me, but all I can really feel is pain, like someone's put a hot iron to my shoulder and kept it there. I can't tell until the mountain's shaking finally stops and the lab we've left behind is sealed in with rocks that I'm screaming.

"Scout!" Kieran's head appears over the edge. He grabs my hand, but at his pull my grip almost slackens, and I know he can't bear all our weight.

"Stop!" I scream.

He does. He looks frantic. Pumpkin arcs dangerously across my chest, the energy of the fall sending him into a pendulum's swing. He yowls and twists, and I can feel him slipping. I can feel *me* slipping.

"Scout." June's voice is commanding, calm. "I'm going to climb up. Hold on."

I want to warn about Pumpkin, but the pain is too much. It washes over me in hot, nauseating waves. When June tugs, I cry out. I'm certain my arm is going to rip off. "Don't," I gasp.

"Scout, focus. Just hold on. For ten seconds, all you have to do is hold on." She pulls her weight up my arm, and I hiss with pain. "This is it, okay? Hold on."

This is it.

The arm I can still feel begins to shake. I realize that if I let go, I'll die. Pumpkin will die. June will die. I realize these might be the last few moments of our lives. But not if I can just hold on.

This is it.

...This one is.

I can really feel my fingers. They are crimped with all the strength I have in me. They are pinching into the ridge layer by layer. My gloves, my skin, my bone, my muscle. And not just the muscles in my hands, but in my forearm, in my biceps, in my still-feeling shoulder. I breathe out.

My pulse thuds in thick, heavy bursts. *Thud thud, thud thud, thud thud.* The static of the electrical storm above me cracks and ripples. I breathe in.

June's weight comes off my dead arm. Her knee presses between my shoulder blades. I grit my teeth with the new pain and turn my head as she presses upward. The horizon is a thin, flat line interrupted frequently by slices of mountainous fangs. They twist intricately, impressively, reaching skyward. I imagine their peaks touched with frost, the pencil-thin river far below full and blue.

A weight comes off my shoulders—literally—and in a flurry of grasping hands, Pumpkin and I are pulled up safely onto the ridge.

21

June's got my arm in a sling, my joint back in its socket. She's pumped me full of something that's cleared the pain and the haze that came with it, and something else that's mending the damaged tissues from the inside. Judging by the ample supply in her open pack, this stuff is standard-issue for Verity Co. It's top tier, and I feel better already. When she draws the sling back, face hardened like a soldier at war, she tells me to rotate my arm. It moves better than it did before the dislocation.

"Thank you," I say, and she nods distractedly, standing slowly and looking out over the wind-whipped mountains.

I give Kieran what I hope is a reassuring look despite how bedraggled I feel. The arm's better, but my heart's still racing, and I can't help looking over my shoulder to where the Stelhari lab has been sealed in by the rocks. Kieran gives me back a harrowed half smile and holds Pumpkin, splayed out like a rag doll, closer to his chest. I look again to the sealed lab. After a few uneasy *settlings*, it's been quiet. The Remnant and its chilling cold are long gone, but the memory of it is like a scar.

After injecting me with Verity Co.'s miracle drug, June contacted her compatriot in orbit: someone named Eileen, who was the one speaking through their dinghy's radio when we arrived. Eileen is fighting to find the small ship's signal so she can remotely and manually route it to our location. During the fight with the Remnant, whatever technology allowed June to warp back to her dinghy was damaged.

It's been a long ten minutes sitting on this thin slice of cliff, but Eileen has assured June she need not worry, that she's working on it. There is an edge of elder kindness to her voice, the nearly indiscernible rumble of age.

I don't ask about her. I don't want to try June's mood. I especially keep quiet about her forgoing mention of Gunner's death. Eileen thinks she's picking up five (including Pumpkin).

It hits me again that he's dead, now that I can think about something other than my arm hanging limply in my skin. I don't care for him personally, but he is—was—a person. He was there one moment and gone the next, just like that. No warning, no ceremony, no chance to say goodbye. Three days ago he was smug and ornery, standing tall on Nebul. Now he's dead.

"I'm sorry," I say, "about Gunner."

June sighs or laughs, and shakes her head. "Yeah."

"The Remnant was bad luck," Kieran adds. "I'm sorry too."

"Not bad luck. We knew it was there. And that's the job."

I frown. "You knew it was there?"

"Yeah, we did. Easy enough, with our scanners." She raps her forearm brace with the backs of her fingers, and my head spins.

Tracking Remnants is impossible. They're as dangerous as they are because of that impossibility. As *lethal* as they are because of that impossibility. But June's not lying.

"Like the warning did us any good," she goes on. "Doesn't matter. We—*I*—got the cache." It hangs off her now, a bulky cylinder strapped against her thigh.

I blink, dumbfounded. Angry.

I'm tired of dealing with Verity Co. I'm terrified of this little slice of rock we're on, dangling over these mountains. I'm a lot of things, but above all I'm worried. Kieran and I didn't get here in time. We didn't get to stumble upon a recorded message, or copy just enough of a cache to find out where we need to go next. If I can't get something out of June...

I suck my lips, staring at that cache, and she catches me. "What?" she snaps.

"Sorry," I say, and I can feel how flat it is, like a layer of concrete over a geyser of anger. She follows my eyes to her thigh.

"Seriously?"

"Look," I say. "I know you're in pain. I know Gunner meant—"

"Stop presuming things. Right now."

I swallow, try again. "What happened to him could happen to so many more. What happened to this *world* could happen to so many more."

She laughs, looks at Kieran. "Is this real? This whole *the universe is in danger and I'm the only one who can save it* shtick?"

Before his hanging mouth can speak, I snap, "I never said I'm the only one who can save it. I just don't think Verity Co. will."

"If there was something in these caches that would stop our civilization from crumbling, you don't think they would use it to save people?"

She has a device that can detect Remnants. She and Gunner had a warning.

I glare at her. "The people who could pay, maybe.

The people *worth* saving. And you know that's how it would work out, don't you?"

She crosses her arms.

"The writing has been on the wall a long time," I say. I can't stop myself now. "Continents have sunk into the ocean. Tsunamis have taken out islands. Whole towns without infrastructure have frozen overnight. Millions have died across all our worlds because people with power refuse to cut their profits to acknowledge the real problems.

"We've known for hundreds of years that we're alone in this universe. We've known for decades that the reason why boils down to the same thing: the Remnants, and whatever caused them. And we've finally—finally!—found a people who knew something about what we're dealing with, about what could come for our own planets at any time, and you want to give that information to the organization who won't take a loss to save an entire moon community from a plague their mishandling caused? Who won't make lifesaving medicine free or—fuck—*affordable*? You want to give it to the people who profit off of suffering?"

Her mouth twitches into a frown. A grimace. Then a sneer. "That's how the world works."

"Screw that. It should be better."

"And I *should* be an empress with a hundred servants, for all the work I've done. Life isn't fair. Who knew?"

"It *could* be better," I say, and I can hear Kieran blow out an anxious breath.

June laughs, mean and mocking. "No, it can't be. You can't actually move a mountain. It's just something people with power say to make idiots like you feel like you can change things."

"Help me change things. You—no." I grit my teeth. "You know what? You're just as selfish. You have scanners that can detect Remnants, the deadliest thing in the known universe, an *impossible* tech."

"Blab about it all you want," June growls. "Verity Co. will deny it."

"Do you know how many Archivists have died to Remnant attacks? How many scientists and would-be colonists? How dare you. How dare you keep that for yourself!"

"Point fingers at Verity Co., not me."

"You *are* them."

"I'm *employed* by them." June's face turns a new edge of angry, dangerous. "And you would have been too."

I scoff. "What?"

"Kyla Vervain of Linlo," she drones, and Kieran and I both jar, because it's my name, my full name, my old name, the one I had and always hated because it was never me. "Signed a contract roughly one year ago to conscript into Verity Co.'s service in exchange for the patent for bodily erosion treatment M19x. Only, the recipient of that medicine never signed, did they?"

Kieran stands up.

I take a step back. "How?"

"Please. We just look at you and see everything Verity Co. has in your profile, public and otherwise. So who was it? Who were you willing to become a hypocrite for?"

Kieran stands between me and her. I let my eyes sink to the ground, where Pumpkin bumps against my heels.

"How about you?" Kieran says. "Who did you sell yourself for?"

June doesn't reply. I can't see their faces, but I can see my brother's shoulders, narrow and tense like his balled-up hands. Static warbles in the dangerous silence between them. And then I hear engines, a low, clean hum. A sleek dinghy appears, sharply angled and black. Time's up.

I'm hollow on the ride to our landing zone. I've felt too much in too short a time, and I've failed. I don't have anything from the cache. All I've done, all Kieran's done, and this is what it's amounted to. Nothing.

Maybe June is right about never really being able to change anything.

"Why did you help us?" Kieran mutters. His voice is low, but the space is small.

There's a long silence. Verity Co.'s dinghy doesn't rattle as badly as ours. Can hardly feel a thing.

"Because," she says. The clipped edge of hate has left her voice. She sounds tired. "You're idiots, but you don't deserve to die."

"Why?" he says, more challenge than question.

"Because we're all..." She scoffs. "Well, why did you help me?"

"Because we're the same. But we only really see that in a crisis, I guess." He sighs. "We're the only ones in this cluster. We need to help each other where we can. So, help us."

"I did help you."

"Yeah? We saved your life."

"I saved yours."

"We saved yours twice over," Kieran says. He takes a breath and lowers his voice again. "You wouldn't have made it through that door without me, and you wouldn't have survived that fall if it weren't for Scout."

"And I could have left you both on that ridge."

"If I hadn't helped you through that door, we might not have even been on that ridge."

"Or you'd be dead too," she says. There's no energy in it.

We're approaching the landing zone. I can see it through the windows.

"You owe us," Kieran says. "And dance around it all

you like, but you know they're right about your employer. Give us the location of the next cache. I mean, what could that really change, right?"

We land. The hatch opens automatically, or at June's instruction on the pilot's dash. She keeps the engines running. Kieran stands. He walks past me with a grim expression and exits, Pumpkin at his heels. My feet are leaden, but I go next. I'm halfway to our dinghy when June calls out to me.

"Casmi," she says, standing in the open hatch. "Colonized meteor in the Gethri system. It's the last cache, the last place the Stelhari tried to escape to."

I turn to her.

"We're even now," she says. "I owe you nothing, and"—she breaks eye contact—"I'm sorry." I can't place her expression. Whatever shift is there happens too fast.

"Thank you," I manage. It's incomplete. It doesn't express what I want, but it's what I have.

Before I can turn fully around, fighting the wind to get aboard, she calls, "Scout, I can't let you have that cache. Just know that."

22

June didn't lie. The destination she named matches up with the star chart in our partial cache copy, and now the *Waning Crescent*'s cockpit window is full of warped light as we speed along to where the Stelhari's final cache waits to be found. I should be happy. But there's an ache that hasn't gone away since that ridge on Galan. I don't know if it's the Remnant, or Gunner dying, or June. Maybe it's the last thing she said to me, that she couldn't let us take that cache. Maybe it's realizing she wasn't lying about that either.

There are likely a million things in the Stelhari's derelict civilization worth uncovering: subjects for architectural studies; geological sampling; whatever non-transmitting, mundane artifacts like art and writing are left to find. But this, the answer to the end of so many worlds? There will be nothing else like this.

"How're you feeling?" Kieran asks. He's in the pilot's chair as usual, staring out toward the pinhole of light at the other end of the spacestream we're ripping through.

I toss up my hands, let them fall. What is there to say, really? His mouth twists grimly and he nods, blows air through his nose. Frustrated? Tired? I can't tell.

"Why did you do it?" I ask.

"What?"

"You think it's pointless, right? We can't beat Verity Co., right? You've been wanting to go home since we left Nebul."

"Are you mad at me for talking to her?"

I'm frustrated. I can tell that much. It's a tightening coil in my chest, pulling my throat taut. "No," I say, but it feels like a yes.

"I knew how important getting to the next cache was for you."

For me. Again.

"And it is," he says, "isn't it?"

I push the heels of my hands to my eyes, try to rub out some of the stress. But this just seems to stoke it. "She's not going to let us take the cache."

"That hasn't stopped you before."

"Well maybe it should have." He looks at me, and I

toss my hands up again. "What's the point? Why are we doing this?"

That coil in my chest tightens so that everything around it feels close to snapping. I'm not good at taking slow breaths at a time like this. I sound like I'm hyperventilating. I *am* hyperventilating. *This one is*, I think in Blyreena's voice, automatically and intrusively, and I shoo it away at once, grit my teeth and will the reminder to pass. But the damage is done.

Bly, I'm sorry.

I'm sorry her words will end up in uncaring hands. I'm sorry her message will fall on deaf ears. I'm sorry her people's legacy will be exploited for profit and greed instead of what she stood for. I'm sorry that everything she and her people did to help might be wasted.

"Scout?" Kieran's looking at me, more grim-faced than before.

"What?"

He sucks his lips and shakes his head. "No, never mind."

"What?" I press.

"This isn't the time for it. Just, never mind."

"Whatever you have to say can't possibly make me feel worse." I catch his grimace, his swallow. I brace myself. "Well, now you have to tell me."

"After this mission," he mutters, "after we get home, I'm going to request a transition to planet-side duty."

I wince like he's hit me, because it kind of feels like he has.

He sighs. "I told you this wasn't the time."

"Why?"

"Because—"

"Is it the Remnant? Something June said?"

"It's a lot of things. I, look, I've been thinking about this ever since we left home. There's not a day I haven't thought about it, even before all this, before we got to this cluster."

"Is it me?"

"No." He turns in his seat to face me. "No, it's not you. Getting to spend time with you has been one of the few good parts of this whole thing."

I turn away from him, toward the stars. They're all lines still, bleeding past like multicolored paint strokes. I try to imagine this life without my brother. I expect it to stir something in me: pain, sadness. But now, after everything, I just feel numb.

"It gets lonely out here," he says, "even with you and Pumpkin. I don't want to die like Gunner, isolated in a part of the universe with only a handful of other people in it. I don't want to die this far from home."

"You're worried about dying, then?"

"I'm worried about—" he starts, but stops, shakes his

head. I'm watching him in the reflection in the glass. "Don't you ever miss other people?"

"Sometimes." But *rarely* might be more truthful.

I love being out in the universe. I love the stars, space, other worlds, the hum of the ship when I sleep. Whenever I'm home, planet-side, it's so easy to get caught up in things. The news. The wars. The economy. Pushing paper, getting promotions, an endless slew of new movies and games and content and products. It's easy to lose sight of the sky, to fall into the pattern of thinking that the only things that matter are the ones I find myself surrounded with. I suffocate back home. Even when Mom was there, I suffocated.

"I do," Kieran says. "I miss my friends. I miss going to pizza places, and not having to ration everything, and not having to worry about an oxygen leak killing me in my sleep. I miss the sounds, even. Just the sounds of other people. Even the noisy transports and construction. I miss being surrounded by life."

I want to retort, but what would it change? I can see, in the way his reflection smiles, in the sudden ease that comes into his face, that he means what he says. He feels deeply about it. His mind is made up.

His reflection faces mine. It's easier to imagine they're other people, those reflections, that I'm not the one whose brother wants to leave them. Just another sad story I get to watch unfold.

"I'm sorry," he says. "I know this isn't what you want to hear. And I know…this wasn't the time to tell you."

"I think I kind of knew," my reflection mutters softly.

He nods, sad-looking again, now that he's seen my face. "But you asked why we're doing this, and it's, well, why I talked to June. For you. I care about these caches, and the fate of our worlds, and answers, but… not as much as you do, sib. It's true. I'm sorry, but it's true. I know you need to see this through all the way to the end. *I* need to see *you* through, all the way to the end. So…" He looks at me and waits until I look at him. No more reflections. "That's my reason," he says. "But I can't be the one to decide yours."

23

Pumpkin follows me from the cockpit to my cabin. I try playing with him, which he at least enjoys. I try listening to music. I try watching a bit of a movie on my own. None of it works. I can't fill in the wound Kieran's given me, and I can't figure out why I've pushed so hard to get to a cache we'll inevitably lose. I don't know what I could have done to change Kieran's mind, and I don't know what I *can* do to change June's. The certainty of his leaving and the uncertainty of what I can do on Casmi are pulling me apart as if from opposite sides, and there's no amount of distraction that can keep me from suffering through it.

It tears me up into frustrated pieces of myself. I can't play with Pumpkin or play a game; and sitting, doing nothing, is a maddening existence, an all-consuming nonfocus that robs me of the ability to do anything but think and think and *think*.

I think about all the things I've done that could have made Kieran want to leave. I think of all the ways I could have stopped June up to this point. I think about how I could have let her die. I think about how if I had, the cache she carried would have been lost. I think about the cache I do have, the partial one, the Stelhari inside it and how earnest she is, how Verity Co. will never see that earnestness. I think about how she said she'd be making her last stand and that I have yet to see what that is. I think that the only thing I can do, right now, to make any difference at all, is finish what I started with the one piece of information I have.

I don't know what it will amount to, or what it's amounted to so far. But it has to be better than doing nothing. It has to be.

Recording Playback 1.0023.498.x

Speaker and Authorizer: Organizer President, Interstel Councilmember Sy. Blyreena Ekstafor

Rotation 2, Mayak Harvest, 3550

Marriage did not slow Ovlan or me down. After a modest honeymoon in Panev's countryside, we returned to the capital and resumed our lives in earnest: him traveling between home and the moon to orchestrate the construction taking place there; me working in the head Organizer's office, striving to broker more leeway from the Financers for education funding.

Over a few short years, we both made significant headway in our careers. Ovlan was promoted to assistant overseer of the moon's vast habitation project, and I was—impossibly, it felt like—advanced to Interstel leadership candidacy. We celebrated over satellite, each drinking straight from bottles of fizz and ordering the same meals, though from very different places. We were enamored with each other's successes.

These advancements in our fields led to a period of time Ovlan and I saw each other very little in person. We called one another every night we could, but we went weeks, sometimes months, without getting to hold one another. We made up for it with remote date nights: movies, shows, cooking contests (with a visual emphasis, of course); we would scour our digital collections for rare joke books, or one-up each other with cuter and cuter pictures of small animals. I missed him terribly, and he missed me, but I never felt like he was far away. I'd open windows and go to sleep, as often as I could, looking up at the moon.

Knowing he was always there, even if not physically, kept me going through countless difficulties at work. As proud as I am to serve, politics, as it is said, is politics. It can be ruthless. Disheartening. There were rivals to my positions, fighting for their own visions for the future, some in good faith with different ideals, others, it seemed to me, for the primary purpose of gaining power, for limiting the rights of others, for stoking time-wasting minutiae on an intersystem level. There was…a particularly difficult day.

I was campaigning for Panev's Interstel seat. A speech had gone over badly in light of news that morning. I was already tired and defeated and unsure of what to say in the face of so much fear and worry, in the impossible certainty of the opposition. It had been a setback, my allies told me, but not an insurmountable one. It certainly felt so.

As insurmountable and unshakable as that long period of unemployment after school? they chastised me. They had all seen Ovlan's gift to me in my office.

I left work late that day, which wasn't terribly unusual, and picked up some late-night dinner from our favorite café beside the lake. I fully intended to tuck back into work after dinner and our usual chat. I booted up our video call system to see that he was away, which wasn't terribly unusual for him either. I ate and checked messages while I waited:

updates on research projects I was involved in, pointers and encouragement from my campaign manager, news from my regular subscriptions. I was surprised to find I had missed two calls since leaving work, both from Panev's Interbody Transportation System, asking me to call them urgently. I had a few projects linked to them and…

Sorry. This is… Excuse me.

I had a few projects linked to them, so I called them straightaway. Even with the late hour, my call was picked up immediately. It began with condolences and ended with them telling me Ovlan was dead.

He had been on a shuttle from the moon to Panev that departed an hour before. There had been a major malfunction in the filtration system. Everyone onboard had suffocated.

I don't remember what I said. I don't remember hanging up. I think I thought it was a wrong-number situation. It couldn't have been my Ovlan. My Ovlan wasn't due home for another week. He was still on the moon, finishing up work, getting ready to call me. I looked at my computer. His status was *Away*. Away, not offline. Away, not dead.

I stared at that little orange crescent symbol. My food went untouched and cold. At some point, I conducted a search.

My fingers shook while swiping through news

alerts. There were pictures. Live feeds. A press conference. There were bodies under sheets.

I came across it either hours or minutes in. I can't remember the time, only the words, a headline: *Assistant Overseer Ovlan Faranawe among Deceased in Juniper Shuttle Malfunction.*

Ovlan. My Ovlan.

Holographic Blyreena hangs her head. She pinches all four lanky fingers on one hand into her eyes. She says sorry, and the image disappears. It reappears moments later with a timestamp five hours later, but I pause. I close my eyes.

I am with Blyreena on Panev. I am in the spire's command center with her during those five hours. She knows her planet is about to be consumed. She knows this is the last thing she will leave behind. She is distressed and afraid about everything happening around her, and she is reliving this pain. For five hours she relives this pain until she can compose herself and begin anew with that calm, centered smile.

I don't know what it is that makes me take this time to think of her grief. I don't know Blyreena. I don't know Ovlan. They have been dead for hundreds of years, but I feel the loss. I know the loss. I've never known a love like they had, and that loss is personal and different, but I think of my mom. I think of what losing my brother would feel like. I think, simply, that

Blyreena was a person who loved someone very much, and he was taken from her.

Even at its core, even without common experience, there is something universal about loss. I can feel it, deep as heartache. Something stirs at loss. Something awakens to it, like a knowing, like an understanding, that this is how everything ends.

24

Recording Playback 1.0023.498.x

Speaker and Authorizer: Organizer President, Interstel Councilmember Sy. Blyreena Ekstafor

Rotation 2, Mayak Harvest, 3550

Have you ever bitten into an apple and tasted nothing? Have you ever caught a favorite song over someone else's broadcast, over the speakers in a shopping outlet, and found that the words that once stirred you now echo hollow in your heart?

There is a moment where you wake up the next day, after two hours' sleep, eyes red and raw, throat red and raw from crying, from begging, where you have forgotten. Where you blink awake and think, so naturally, so rhythmically, *Today I work; today I eat; today I call Ovlan.* And then it hits you all over again, wave after wave of helplessness, a hot blade to every string of your soul that connects you to meaning.

You think to move, to crawl, to pace. Hurt is a thing you can outrun, you think, but you can't. You leave a trail of tears that follows you from bed to toilet to kitchen. Your knees ache from where you've crawled on them, where, when trying to walk, you've collapsed on them. Your body has given up. You have cried so hard there is nothing left to spill. Water burns, your mouth is so parched.

There are messages for you, waiting. A thousand of them. Friends, family, Father, Dad, mother-in-law, sister-in-law, but not Ovlan. Not the one person you are hoping beyond anything in the cosmos to see. You stare at the messages and wait; you wait for the cameras to reveal themselves, to proclaim that it was all an elaborate prank, that it was a test of love to see how much your heart would break. Because spirits, it is broken. It is shattered like a grenade, and the shrapnel is bleeding you from the inside.

We're coming, the messages say. Your parents are coming. Your friends are coming. *Hold on,* they say, but they will be too late. There will be nothing of you by the time they arrive.

You lie face down on the cool marble floor and will yourself to sleep. To sleep is to wake, you think. This is a nightmare. You have had many nightmares; they all feel so real until the moment you wake up. So you beg yourself to wake up. You pinch yourself, you close your eyes, you refresh the messages, the news, the obituaries; you scour the world for a thread of reality to grasp on to like a drowning person reaching for a rope. You stare at your communicator. *Any minute now,* you think, and you believe it with all your heart. *Any minute now, he'll call.*

But it is not Ovlan who comes to your door, only your family—blood and otherwise. They scoop you into their arms like you are a wounded animal, and like a wounded animal, you give up. Your last shred of hope dies with their being there, because they would not come for anything else, they would not whisper *We are so sorry* and *It will be okay* and *We're here, Blyreena, we're here* if Ovlan were alive. You go limp with their condolences. You stare out the window across the lake, and the blue sky looks gray. There is no music in the birdsong. There is nothing left to feel but empty.

When Mom died, I was at the Archivist Academy Library. I had gone there thoughtlessly, out of a need for momentum. I had just left her at the hospital. I'd been mad at her.

I got the call in the courtyard, inside the shadow of the spired main building. I paused on the first step and answered. I said nothing when the news hit. I think I had gone straight to empty from the start.

Mom had never been afraid to die, but I'd been terrified of losing her. I'd been fearing it for weeks. I'd been answering every call ready for the worst. And when it finally was the worst? I hung up, tearless, and went inside the library.

Blyreena's loss was shrapnel. Mine was a scoop you cored fruit with.

Grief is an oscillation. There were little moments, hours, days, where things would seem normal. I would be watching a show with my father and laugh, or making dinner with my best friend, Elise, and ask her—out of habit, out of interest, out of love, as natural as breath—how her own life was going. I would get well-meaning, encouraging smiles and nods, under which the subtle surprise at my calm would stab like a grim reminder.

There were moments, hours, days, where I would become as I had the first time I heard the news. Inconsolable. Empty. Torn and shredded from within, with everything spilling out of me. These moments would happen for no reason at all or because I would see my bed and remember: *Ovlan will never lie here again.* Or I would see nothing but feel an excitement, a self-betrayal, a: *I can't wait to tell him about this funny thing Dad did. He'll think it's hysterical.* Joy turned to shrapnel.

In the days leading up to his death rites, I could not sleep. My own self-interests turned instead to him, the man I loved with all my being. Had he been scared? Did he see the malfunction as it happened? Did he gasp at that first intake of breath that would not come, that would not supply him the means to breathe? How long did he try to hold on? Did it hurt? Was anyone there a comfort to him? Was he a comfort to someone else? What were his last thoughts? Why had he been there at all? Why did he board that shuttle a week early?

Why, Ovlan? Why?

Mom had tried to explain, but her reasons didn't make sense to me. Her will was indomitable. Unmoving. What could I have done in the face of it? And yet, why didn't I do more?

The *Waning Crescent* rumbles. The lines of light outside shift and disperse, twinkle away into pinprick stars. We've left jump space. I think about Casmi, about June, about Verity Co., about that last cache. I think about leaving with nothing but the memory of having let something so precious slip from my grasp.

After Ovlan's rites, after my dad and father affirmed and reaffirmed with me that I could make it on my own, and my bursts of grief had become manageable, I entered back into my life. Elise left. My parents left. I listened to their footsteps until they were gone. I watched them out the window, waved when they looked up before their transports carried them away. I turned back to an empty apartment that no one was planning to come back to without an invitation. I was alone.

This bore the kind of striking grief that feels like a slap anew. I could not help but see the slight indents in the couch where Ovlan and I sat, or the chair he favored at the table, or his clothes still in the closet. I was not ready to say goodbye to these things. They alternated between offering comfort and pain.

In the absence of company, I pored over his things methodically. Every robe, every drawing, every blueprint. His degree, his journal, the daily planner on his tablet. I sifted through the meetings he'd had, the notes he'd taken. I read archives of our chats, relived every saved moment from our ten years together, trying to fall into them. I would have given anything—would still give anything—for one last chat. One last hello. The opportunity to tell him goodbye and tell him that he changed the world for me, that he made it brighter and better than anything else ever could.

I was so lost chasing this reality that could not exist, mourning a future that had been erased, a past that could never be reclaimed. I would have been adrift forever, but…

Two days after my family left, I received a package from the Nurturer's End of Life Division. Builder policy encouraged active workers on Ilvi 10 to make arrangements due to the inherent danger in the work. Though it hadn't been officially filed, the division had found a recording in Ovlan's personal station. His last stand.

It had been recorded well before the last words he'd ever speak but with all the intention of a final goodbye. A final gift to the universe he would eventually leave behind.

What he said… I watched it many times. Sank into it. Breathed with it in grief and relief at seeing something new, at hearing his voice around words I'd not heard him speak, compounding with each viewing. It's what finally opened the door back into something like living. It's what allowed me not to move on but to give in to the grief, to understand it.

It's what allowed me, days later, when I finally returned to work, to enter my office and laugh. I had arrived to the grim but expected news that my campaign had fallen through, that my opponent in my absence had advanced to the Interstel candidacy I'd sought. My peers worried at my laughter, but I'd laughed because the first thing I saw upon entering that office after so long, after so much awful news over so many months, was the framed thesis review Ovlan had given me so long before.

Between it and his last stand, I really understood. *Things have a way of working out,* I thought, and it was like he was there in the room. Things had never looked bleaker, getting that review (things had never looked bleaker, standing in that office, my partner dead, my campaign ruined), but *here I stand.* Here I am now.

This one is, he would say.

Ovlan…

He was young, too young, tragically young. But he had so much to teach me. Us. He loved me, but his wisdom was not reserved for me. He lived his life in a way that made the people around him shine brighter. I've had to say goodbye to so many of those people: his parents, my parents, friends; and now I will have to say goodbye to this world. To our home.

Standing here, knowing full well that our civilization may be at its end, I can think of no better words to hear—or to share—than Ovlan's. For myself, for any Stelhari who may come to recover this cache, victorious, or...for whoever comes after.

To whoever is listening to this, or translating it word by word, or reading its transcript, know that this last piece of wisdom I have of his to share, this last gift...

It is for you.

I stare at Blyreena's paused hologram. I am too much in shock to know whether Kieran has pinged me or not about our arrival. I have been viewing her last stand wrong. Like so many things, it is an issue of translation.

Our machines have a million points of decision for picking the right word or phrase to match alien text and speech, and even those million can fail to capture the specificity intended. It's easy because of this to draw erroneous similarities between us and another species, a simple fact of our language being superimposed over theirs.

In my culture, in my tongue, a last stand is a final effort to defend oneself. A last bulwark against the enemy. I have made the most basic and most insidious of archeological mistakes. It cannot be helped. I do not beat myself up for it. But I understand. I cross-compare with the notes I've taken, the historical records. It is so innocuous; they did not spell it out, but the lines have been drawn. I add a dictation to the recording where I've paused, where Blyreena is staring at me, a soft smile on her face.

Last Stand: Usually part of Stelhari death rites. It is not a stand—defensively—but a stance. A position. The last one they give to their loved ones, or the world, before they die.

I resume the video and watch as Blyreena brings up another hologram, of a man—of Ovlan.

I listen to everything he says twice.

25

Unlike Panev, Nebul, or Galan, Casmi is a meteor, home to what the few records we have label as a research facility for studying the system's dying sun. It is a dull red thing now, that sun, hundreds of thousands of kilometers away and fading still. Casmi itself is large for a meteor, oblong, jagged, and pocked with craters. There are long ridges of rock that wind for several kilometers, marred with caves and tunnels, and tall enough that they are like mountains. In the valley of their shadows sits a cluster of domes like cracked, fissured boils. A bubble city, something that allowed the Stelhari to live here, and just like all their worlds that came before, dead.

It becomes clearer as Kieran steers the dinghy downward. There stands a central dome with five equidistant offshoots connected by arched tunnels. The domes are translucent, massive structures, the central one standing twice as high as the rest. Every one of them is damaged: cracked, splintered, melted, shattered. Only one dome can be considered anything close to intact. Its outer reinforced glass is shattered like all the others. Large shards of it have fallen away and pierced the ground. But within the remains of the destroyed structure, filling it from the inside like an additional shell, is a gunmetal dome. It is uncracked, unmarred, unbroken. It is where the *Waning Crescent*'s sensors have picked up a cache.

Kieran lands us in the central dome, where wide pathways flanked by empty, destroyed planters have left an abundance of space. We both brace for a proximity alert because we both know June must be here. But no alarm triggers.

Our dinghy lands. The engines hiss, releasing heat. Our belts unbuckle, and our boots rap against steel, then stone as we exit. Pumpkin goes right to a planter whose outer wall has ruptured outward, spilling dry, crumbly dirt. He sniffs through his helmet.

We're in what must have been a sort of dual-purpose park. The planters seem more aesthetic than functional with their oblong-to-sharp-angle shapes, but broken, complex tubing showing beneath the dirt suggests hydroponics. I push the brittle earth aside to reveal more of the weaving tubes. Their trails go under the foundations of the planters, but there are no water tanks—not inside the planters, not outside them. The tubes dive under the floor and vanish.

I check the tracker, locking on to the *Waning Crescent*'s scanners and the cache signal they're tracking. It's still there, in the metal dome up ahead. I lead the way.

Pumpkin and Kieran fall into step beside me. Our footfalls tap and scrape across the walkways, accented only by our breathing. The system's red sun wavers above our heads, only twice the size of all the glittering stars around it. Our headlights cast long, pale shadows.

I step around a stone bench, cracked and tumbled. There is no doubt in my mind that this facility is similar to the kind Ovlan helped construct on Panev's moon. A habitable community in dangerous terrain, built for the Stelhari's premier scientists. A research station on the fringes of their civilization. All that importance, all the danger inherent in living on a meteor, and they dared to build a park. They dared to make it beautiful.

"You okay?" Kieran asks. "You're quiet."

"I'm fine," I say, but not in the passive-aggressive way it's sometimes meant. "Just thinking."

We have to split apart, maneuver around a half-meter-thick shard of collapsed dome. We come back together on the other side.

"About last night," he says, "about me going home—whoa!" He trips and stumbles. Pumpkin rushes to bop him helpfully as he stands and dusts himself off. "Whoops."

"You alright?"

"Yeah—yep."

I smile at his nervous stutter. "Let's just focus on getting through here without tripping and dying, okay? We can talk about all that later."

He nods and motions for me to lead the way through the narrow path before us.

After a little accident-free maneuvering, we reach the tunnel that leads to the gunmetal dome. A steel computerized door, linked to a familiar control panel on the frame, is busted open from our side. It is shorn in two, with one half shredded on the floor two meters inside the tunnel. Pumpkin glides bravely under the tattered remains of the door still attached and sniffs the new terrain.

Halfway through the tunnel, the steel floor is sunken for about twenty meters, like a sinkhole with jagged rebar teeth. I stand at the edge. There's darkness below through the gaps between steel and foundation, but my headlight catches more steel, more pathways, a structure beneath the ground. The cave-in has made a mess of both that path and this one up here.

It takes time, testing, and wiggling Pumpkin into the straps of my suit, but enough of the floor still remaining is sufficient for us to navigate across with a simple support line anchored to the intact tunnel walls. There are no sinkholes the short rest of the way, only a collapsed piece of tunnel ceiling, through which a shard of the shattered dome up ahead is impaled. The shard's thick, pointed end is stuck halfway through like a fang.

I think about the Remnant on Galan, about how it couldn't—or didn't—burst through the rubble June had made with her bomb to catch us. Whatever it was a Remnant *of*, though—the Endri—it didn't have problems with walls or destruction. The glass shard is thicker than my forearm. It rings solid when I rap it with my knuckles.

The door at the end of the tunnel leading into the next dome is ripped completely off the frame, bent oddly and left to the side. But just past the frame, immediately blocking the entrance, is that gunmetal dome. This close up, it's layered like an armadillo's shell, like a phalanx of ancient shields. There are surface scrapes and tears but no meaningful punctures. It's very cool to the touch, even through my suit. I let Pumpkin out of the straps to explore.

Kieran approaches the dome and knocks.

"Seriously?" I say.

"June could be in there."

"I don't think she'd answer if she was."

"Well, then this is going to be difficult." He feels around the base of the shield with both hands. The whole thing is pressed within centimeters of the forearm-thick glass, perfectly constructed to fit inside the dome that was.

"Why?"

"See here? These slots? The way this thing is layered, it looks like it was sprung—activated—and came up from a launch point within the ground."

A not-unfamiliar mechanism, though usually the sorts of automated defenses I've seen are energy-based. Plasma shields. Force-emitting barriers. I nod.

"If this was computerized or otherwise electronically activated," he continues, "like most of the tech we've seen in Stelhari territory, then it's likely controlled from inside."

I look back through the tunnel at the rest of the compound. "How can you be so sure?"

"There's only one of these." He jerks his chin to the shell and slips his pack off to dig around inside it. "Kind of reminds me of the emergency bunkers back home. Get everyone in one place, lock it down from the inside." He pulls out the hilt of a hot-breach blade. "Stand back?"

I do and make sure Pumpkin comes with me. He meows with distaste, but as Kieran activates the breaching tool, unleashing the spring-loaded blade, he backs up even farther than me. The blade turns bright orange with carefully contained heat at the flip of the safety switch, and Kieran presses the tip into the shell. It punctures, but then he stops, like he's hit a stronger wall. The blade begins to lose its glow from the tip, like the heat is being sucked out of it.

Environmental hazard alerts appear on the insides of our helmets, warning us about the sudden heat radiating off the object in front of us. It's absorbing both the heat and color of Kieran's blade. He pulls it out with more force than I was expecting and falls into me with the effort, knocking us both to the floor.

Pumpkin hisses. The shell returns to its gunmetal color.

"Almost lost it," Kieran says, rolling to his feet. He worries over the tool, twisting it in his grip while looking for damage.

I cautiously rub the tiny nick on the shield where his blade went through. "That did practically nothing."

"Yeah, I saw that." He retracts the blade into the hilt and goes to his pack again. "I'll try the acid next."

He applies the toxic yellow paste via a remote injector with a shielded head to prevent backsplash. He's got the neutralizer at the ready just in case some gets on him anyway, and Pumpkin and I are much farther back than we were for the blade. This stuff is powerful enough to melt fortified steel. I don't even like having it on the ship, but Kieran insists it's safe so long as it stays in its dispenser.

The acid barely even erodes the color of the shell, turning the gray only slightly greenish. It definitely doesn't eat the metal away or reveal a hole or hollow point for us to crawl through or work with. He tries the blade again anyway, stabbing it into the off-color patch. Predictably, it does nothing at all.

"We could try blasting it with the dinghy's weapons," he says, exhausted with the effort.

Those things are paltry and Kieran knows it. I shake my head. "I don't think we have forty years to bust in there. And June's not here, which means she found another way in."

"There's no other way in. The shield goes all the way around."

I look outside. It's just meteor around the dome. No air supply, water tanks, food silos, which would all be a problem if people were trying to survive inside. Food, they could have stocked. But air? Water? They wouldn't have erected a shield just to die in a few days. There have to be vents, water systems, something that would have given them life for just a little longer. I think about the hydroponic tubes in the planters, the path below the sunken tunnel.

"I think I might know a way in," I say and lead the way back to the central dome.

26

We find a claustrophobic cluster of massive life-support systems in the southernmost dome. Recycled air and water tanks are half-burrowed in the ground like root vegetables. Some of their hulls are torn open, cut into from the outside. There's no water left in any of them, and sensors show no breathable air, either, for any species. Although the bottoms have small, grate-covered draining tubes, they're so narrow that only Pumpkin would be able to make it through. Neither I nor Kieran are eager to volunteer him.

But we find our shot in a small, unassuming building at the back of the dome, hidden behind the forest of tanks, tubes, and scaffolding. Kieran does his thing with the door to break it open, and inside, down a hatch, is the entrance to a labyrinthine web of maintenance tunnels. A map engraved into the wall beside the hatch details their paths through the entire compound under every dome.

"This looks familiar," Kieran says. "Like the maps underground in Nebul."

The hatch is already open. It's a ten-meter drop to the floor below, where the remains of the ladder lay scattered. I crouch and pat Pumpkin's back, dissuading him from a leap of faith. Kieran pulls out an image-capture device and scans the map. He hums disapprovingly and tries again.

"What's up?" I stand to get a look at the screen he's offering me.

Archivist image-capture devices are good tech, bolstered by artificial intelligence that cleans up and enhances images to make them clearer. They'll fill in marred material with like material around it, smooth out blurs, and—essentially like our hindsight modules—attempt to recreate the image that was, rather than the one that is. A useful thing for studying the ancient history of dead civilizations.

But in this case the map is so marred—burned here, scuffed there, chipped on the corners—that the enhancements haven't done much. Chunks of the map are lost or, in one quadrant, badly guessed by the AI. Guesses are acceptable when looking at a piece of art, but not a map. It has created lines in mimicry of the ones clearer elsewhere, but the paths are obviously incorrect.

I touch the map in the wall, rub my fingers over paths concealed by scorches but not by touch. I smile to myself.

"What?" Kieran says.

"You'll see." He's confused at my smugness, and I can't help but string him along. I finally get to do the most archaic thing in an archeologist's toolkit. I pull a thin square packet from my bag and open it, taking out the pen—yes, pen—gas-charged and space-safe, as well as a single large sheet of paper.

Manual writing instruments have been around since we were making tools out of extra-hard dirt, but the technology fell into serious disuse a millennium ago. Until, that is, Archivists discovered that some artifacts and monuments had a reflective element that made image capturing impossible, or at least woefully incomplete. Some, bafflingly, even resisted scans. Other worlds, especially in the Centurion Cluster, prominent in the great Archivist-managed expedition that took place before I was even born, had purely mechanical traps—no detectable electronics—that would activate at the presence of any light, even infrared (the explorer's diaries about that cluster are a must-read for any archeologist).

So the Archivists went old, *old* school, deep into the

history books, and revived the lost art of rubbings. Rubbings can't capture smooth surfaces or giant statues made of mud, but embossed surfaces?

I shear the paper down to size and press it against the map. "Hold this?"

Kieran does, and I gently glide the pen across the paper. It looks like nothing at all at first, but as I draw wider swaths across the page, the lines begin to show: all the little details, tiny gaps, chips, and missing pieces, the intensity of the jutting metal in some places and the subtlety in others. I can feel myself smiling.

"You're such a nerd." Kieran laughs, bemused or bewildered, or both. "Stop taking your time with it. It's...weird."

"It's not weird. It's a process."

"It's kind of weird."

"Meow," Pumpkin says.

"You can't rush this," I say. When I'm done, I put the pen away while Kieran observes my handiwork.

"This will work," he says.

I cross my arms. "That's it?" That was the coolest thing I've ever done.

"That's it." He sounds dismissive, but he's grinning.

We set up an anchor and descender, not wanting to brave the drop without aid. I wonder if June has already come this way. There's been no sign of her yet, but I know she's here. This is the last cache the Stelhari left us. She's not going to give us even the slightest upper hand.

Kieran magnetizes the anchor with a switch, then loops the cord through it and around the hefty hatch handle for emergency support. At last, he drops the cord down the hole.

"You first?" he says.

I strap Pumpkin in, and down we go.

The tunnel below is spacious. There's more than enough room to stand in, which makes sense, given the Stelhari species averaged six centimeters taller than ours. It's also plenty wide enough for us to walk two across. The path runs north toward the central dome, and sans a few diverting routes, seems mostly to follow the contours of the bubble city above. Behind us, just beneath the life-support dome, is a cistern. All the tanks that are resting partly beneath the floor show through here, with powered-down panels and complex tubing leading from them to the walls, where they trace snakelike up and down every corridor that I can see.

Seeing nothing dangerous, I let the struggling Pumpkin out of his straps.

Kieran drops down and brings the whole descender with him, anchor and all. We lost a full set back on Galan. Now we only have three left. That's another full backup, but on months-long excursions through space, the loss of even one critical supply feels like losing a limb. We're not risking losing another one unless we absolutely have to.

I lead the way with the copied map stretched tightly between my hands. Kieran walks right beside me, tracing his finger across the page. "So there's this main path," he says, "but a lot of smaller maintenance tunnels too." He taps his thumb beside the mark for the metal-encased dome we're walking toward. "It looks like this offshoot here could get us there."

"Let's start with the main path."

"Isn't it blocked, though?"

I squint at the map as we pass a door leading into one of those myriad smaller maintenance routes. "Maybe not entirely. And it's not a long way back to the smaller route between these walls if it is."

"You just want to avoid the squeeze."

"If at all possible, yes." In addition to disliking heights, I'm slightly claustrophobic. And after what happened on Galan, I want a quick exit route.

We stop at Kieran's insistence to examine one of these tighter spaces anyway, a path that leads narrowly—it looks like—through a series of sewer lines beneath the dome containing housing facilities. It's definitely a tight squeeze. On the whole, it appears the main cavernous paths serve as a way to reach these tighter, more specialized places, as well as to deliver air, water, and sewage throughout the compound. The massive color-coded tubes running alongside us are all empty now. Some are intact, but most are broken and hanging, punctured and scorched.

We proceed along the main path. Pumpkin stays close to us, alert with his tail straight up. We pass an open door, one whose specialized spaces connect to the other, narrower route that can get us to the shielded dome if the main path doesn't work out. I keep Kieran moving. We pass a closed door shortly after, the *official* entrance to that narrow space. He tries the door—"Out of curiosity," he says—and finds it locked.

"Can we please just stay on the main path?" I plead. "We're almost there."

"Just keeping options open," he says.

We finally reach the point we can see the collapsed tunnel. It's more of a mess down here than up there. Floor and ceiling and structural supports have caved in, filling the path ahead with sharp, mangled detritus. We stop at the edge of the pile, a step away from where a bent and pointed slice of metal juts out like a threat. Whatever happened here was so significant that even this level's floor is cracked and sunken downward, leaving a several-meter-drop fall into dark, untainted meteor.

There's a magnetized bolt anchor on what remains of the right wall. A cord is strung through it, leading over the gap and through a narrow space left by the collapse.

Kieran looks at me, opening his mouth to speak, and there's a scraping shift on the other side of that gap. We flash our headlights toward it and freeze. Pumpkin readies to bolt.

"June?" I call. Kieran looks at me, agape.

There's no answer, but the scraping stops.

"That is you, right?" I say. "Your anchor has a little *V* on it."

"You are the most persistent Archivist I know," June says. She's muffled by the distance and debris, but I think I can still hear a heavy sigh.

"How did you get through there?"

The scuffing recommences. "Sheer will," she calls, voice strained with exertion.

No will could get a bulky spacesuit through a gap like that, sheer or otherwise. It's so narrow I kind of wonder if even without the helmet and pack I could make it through. Judging by the resumed sounds of climbing, I doubt June is going to give us any hints. And now that I know she's here, and close, the pressure to move faster is mounting.

"She has to have taken off her helmet at least." Kieran is shaking his head at the jungle of sharp metal. "There's no other way, not without risking a rupture."

I do not like that risk at all. Knowing Verity Co.,

they probably have some secretive technology that keeps their operatives alive in abnormal pressure and air environments or something. All I really know for a fact is that we *don't*.

I gesture to the map and point to our alternative route. I don't dare speak in case June overhears us and, I don't know, blows up the other entrance.

When we're far enough away, back at the sealed door Kieran tested before, I look back to where June's probably still climbing. We have to beat her there. *We have to.*

It doesn't take long for Kieran to finish his task. Despite bearing the same evidence of catastrophe we've seen everywhere else, the door is intact enough that when he jump-starts the circuitry, it slides up with relatively few grinding sounds. I think I might hear June calling out during the slide. Not an endangered sound, but a vaguely echoing demand, like she wants to know if we're still lagging behind, or if she should cut the cord so we can't follow her. Maybe it's just an odd reverberation effect from the door. Whatever it is, I want to press on quickly.

On the other side of the door is a small antechamber with two paths marked by color-coded frames. One leads left to the connecting room Kieran mentioned before, and the other leads—hopefully unimpeded—to the shielded dome where the cache resides.

There's a coolness to the air too, biting even through the suit. And there, caught in my headlamp, a layer of frost glittering on the far wall.

Like oil on water.

Like eyes.

And I remember that June can detect Remnants, that this would have been the easier path.

"Kieran." My throat strangles the word, and beside me, Pumpkin yowls deep in his throat. Somehow, both sounds are hollow. The shadows move oddly in the antechamber. "Come here."

My brother frowns, an agonizingly slow gesture as the gears start ticking. They tick too late.

The frigid air, once expelled on the draft of the opening door, now sucks inward, creates currents around my calves. Darkness peels off the wall like stickers, leaving an impossible absence of shadows where my still-shining light should cast them. The dark falls weightless to the ground and, with the cold, sucks inward into one bulging, star-dotted mass. Amorphous and ghastly, the Remnant shivers and swoops forward.

27

We turn and flee. We know that if we are not fast enough, we will die; if we are not decisive enough, we will die; if we are not lucky enough, we will die. I am moving so quickly that everything is blurring. Or maybe it's simply the pitting, gutting fear, but all the same I am thinking in sharp clarity: *we will die, we will die, we will die.* We are running for our lives. We are a trio of souls who just want to live, and the twitching, seething entity behind us wants us to end instead.

We run back down the main path, away from June and the shielded dome and the collapse. Pumpkin is yowling like an alley cat in a fight. His tail whips around like a propeller as he zooms ahead of me, and he's breathing so hard that the defogging agent on the inside of his helmet can't keep up. Kieran is behind me somewhere. I can't see him.

I look back, slow a little. The Remnant spills toward us, rushing through the wide hallway like an ocean wave, like a slice of the night sky turned treacherous liquid. It warps as it moves, twisting light and shadow wrongly, impossibly, its bulging starlike boils swirling like eyes in the glittering black of its mass. It is unlike anything I have ever seen, and it is just behind my brother.

I call his name. It is shrill and scared and young-sounding.

"Go!" he cries back. Somehow he sounds much stronger than me. "Don't stop!"

Pumpkin darts right, off the main path. I dig my heels into the ground to turn in time to follow him. He's gone into the open doorway we saw before, the one that leads back to the chamber we found the Remnant in. There's a path going right to do so, but Pumpkin has found the top left corner of this new room and curled into a shivering ball.

Kieran yells at me; I yell back for him to keep going. I reach out to my cat, but he looks up, spots something in the doorway. I can see it, reflected there in his helmet. I can see the Remnant reaching out to us.

Pumpkin skitters out from under my grasp and bolts after Kieran. The cold is spreading across my back like a glacial wind, but I follow. My fingers are going numb, but I duck and weave through the narrow, damaged space, my helmet scraping against walls as I push, fast as I can.

Ahead, my brother exits the path into the antechamber. He looks back. Pumpkin and I are just behind him, so Kieran runs right, back to the main hall. He shouts something. Ahead, Pumpkin leaps through the final obstacle to follow. But he catches. Stops. There's a pop, and a hiss—not a cat's hiss. He dangles from a piece of jagged, exposed wall, his feet drooping beneath him.

No.

I reach him, step around him into the antechamber so that I have more leverage. He kicks his feet, whines. The Remnant is right there. My fingers are so numb. I grab Pumpkin around the middle and can hardly feel the pressure.

"Scout!" my brother screams. He is in the doorway to the main hall. June is there with him. Her eyes are wide with surprise. Every grenade and weapon and device on her body is primed in neon light.

Pumpkin meows, pleading. I lift with what strength I have left, but the ragged metal has hooked his suit deep. The Remnant advances. It's lunging. But I will not leave Pumpkin behind. I will not let his last memory be me walking away, his last thought be: *Why did they leave me?*

I will not let him feel what I felt when Mom left.

The Remnant reaches out. June and Kieran yell something, maybe—I can hardly tell from the rushing in my ears. I tug. Pumpkin comes free with another pop, another hiss, and I curl around him as I tumble backward and fall. He's shaking badly. He buries his helmeted face in my shoulders, and I think, with the last of my sensation, that I can feel him relax.

Maybe this is worth it. Maybe this small, last comfort is what's important. He's not alone—I'm not alone—when the Remnant engulfs us.

Kieran's cry echoes off the antechamber walls. It is pain expunged. Scout has frozen up like Gunner did; eyes rolling back like Gunner's did. Pumpkin's too.

June hurls something neon that beeps. Fires something else—too fast to catch—from something bulky, something that was once Gunner's. Scout, Pumpkin—they're swallowed by a blue, shimmering light, then an explosion, by a sound like a sonic detonator, a withdrawn *whom*, as if coming from underwater. It shakes the room so badly that Kieran almost falls. June has braced herself in the doorframe.

What remains is dust and raining rock and metal. No Remnant. No Scout. No Pumpkin.

"No," he whispers.

June gets him up. She is urgent and strong. The far

wall of the antechamber has collapsed inward. Something shifts within the rubble of the antechamber, but she drags him along toward the path she was taking before, drags him until he can walk on his own.

They are not pursued.

28

There was a blue-white light. An explosion. Something hit me hard enough to send me flying through an already-crumbling wall. I think maybe I blacked out.

I open my eyes to a narrow passageway filled with dust and debris. The walls are close together. Pipes are exposed. Behind me is a mountain of still-settling detritus completely blocking off some other side. Ahead, the dark, tight corridor stretches well beyond the meager, flickering light of my headlamp. I'm seeing all this through a significant crack in my helmet. I know it's not split all the way through, because, while I'm not top of the class in engineering, I know that if it were, I'd be choking on my last breath. The air does feel thinner, though.

Somewhere in the dark, Pumpkin meows. I twist to

see him and groan at the pain in my side, my head—everything. He's close to me, lying against rubble, panting. There's a tear in his suit that has ruptured his oxygen supply. I focus, and the ringing in my ears gives way to the persistent hiss of not only his tank, but—I wince, looking over my shoulder—mine.

Our suits are lightly armored, especially around the vital bits, but whatever we survived—the Remnant, that explosion—ripped right through. Pumpkin might even be dead if I hadn't been curled around him when whatever happened, happened.

"It's okay," I gasp. The air is definitely thinning. He meows meekly, and I see the haze in his eyes. We're both suffocating.

I have to roll over to get to my pack. The crumbling rubble beneath me shifts and scatters. My pack is slashed through and slightly singed. There are two spare oxygen packs—too bulky to have fallen through the tear—but one has a puncture, a nick of bad fate. It is hissing like Pumpkin and I are hissing.

I search for sealant, a patching kit, but it's missing. My bag of seeds is missing. Some spare food packs are missing. All lost in the heat and the force of that explosion.

The full, sealed oxygen tank suddenly weighs more than a ship.

Pumpkin looks at me. He meows.

★★★

I walked into Mom's hospital room, full of hope. I'd signed the contracts, received my assignment, due to start in a week. That would be enough time to see the tables turned. The treatment, if effective (and it was certified to be, or my contract would be cut in half, guaranteed), would halt the erosion in its tracks in a few days, making room for the costly stem-cell rejuvenation treatment I had also signed some of my years over for. It was all worth it. I would have my mom back. She'd be around for Kieran's graduation, for birthdays, holidays, everything. She'd have another two hundred years.

I walked in, expecting smiles. A nurse administering the first treatment. My mom upright, grateful, brimming with tears and pride.

But there was no nurse when I arrived. No tiny vial of patented medicine guaranteed to save my mom's life. My mom was there, yes, but only brimming with tears and pride. She was lying on her back, the ventilator still over her mouth, her eyes watery and pale, her skin even more papery than the day before. Pumpkin looked up from the foot of her bed and yawned.

"Hey!" I was all smiles, thinking myself just a little early. I pulled up a chair and sat at her bedside, gave her loyal cat guardian a scratch. "Did you get the news?"

Mom took my hands and squeezed. She was all smiles

too. She coughed, and pressurized suction within her mask sucked the traces of blood down a separate tube than the oxygen was coming in through. "I did. They came with the documents an hour ago."

I felt my smile falter. She spoke level and smooth and with gravity, like she was building toward something. Something unpleasant. "Mom." I was angry. Right away, I was angry.

"You have no idea," she said, "what it means to me. How brave you are, my Scout."

"Why?" How could she? What had she been thinking? "I'll get them back in here."

"I won't sign it."

"It's your life, Mom, it's—"

"Your life."

"What?" I remember thinking, *She's insane. It's started. It's in her brain now. She has hours. Minutes.*

"It's *your* life." She reached out for the hands I'd torn away and squeezed them again.

"It's a few years—"

She laughed. Not bitter, but knowing; not pitying, but sad. "Sweetheart," she said, "I want you to listen very carefully. I'm okay with what's happening."

I ripped my hands away again. I couldn't believe—couldn't handle—anything I was hearing.

"I'm not happy, mind you. I wish it were different. I wish I could be out in the world with you and Kieran and not in this damn bed. And I'm scared. Every night I'm scared, every day. But it's okay. I've accepted it. I have you here to see me. Your brother comes to see me." She coughed. And coughed. And coughed. The pressurized tube became, for a moment, a thick river of blue, congealed blood. "But I will be damned if I let them take your life from you so I can live a few more years."

"It's more than a few years, Mom. It could be an entire life."

"The treatment is perpetual—"

"And I've signed the time for it—"

"You haven't," she said, with such certainty that I could not counter. "Once you're indentured, they will not let you go. The treatments will need to become more frequent. The medicine will change—"

"You don't know that."

"I absolutely do."

I scoffed. "Then it's worth it. Who cares?"

"I do."

"But I don't. And it's my time, my life. I get to choose how to spend it."

"Not if you give it away." She tried to sit up, but another fit of coughing took her. I held her hand as it subsided. "Your life is yours. Sweetheart, listen. You only get one shot at it, but..." She looked to the ceiling, dazed. "What a shot mine has been. I have lived one hundred and twenty amazing years. I have traveled to exoplanets, discovered artifacts, studied other civilizations."

"Mom."

"My life has been—and that's the thing, my love, my child—*every* life has been—"

"Please." I was crying. She was justifying why I should let her die. Because she'd lived? Because she'd lived longer?

"We don't get to choose how long we're here for," she said. "We don't get to choose the circumstances we find ourselves in, a lot of the time. And let me tell you, some people, they find themselves in quite the doozies. Some people, they're treated like less than dirt from the start. But Scout. Scout, listen to me. Sweetheart, please. Look at me. Listen to me."

Pumpkin's tank is replaced.

No more hissing for him. No more suffocating. He's a smart little guy, but dim enough he can't say no, dim enough he can't see that there's only one lifesaving little tube, not two. There's a persistent warning on my helmet now, telling me I'm running out of air, that things are about to get critical.

The path ahead is cluttered with debris. It is wide enough for me to squeeze through, barely, and twists away into the darkness. I don't know where it leads. I don't even know which way is up. But there's no going back through the rubble behind us.

Maybe Pumpkin senses something is wrong, because he takes one look at me having to try twice to get up and decides to lead the way.

Recording Playback 1.0023.498.x

Speaker and Authorizer: Organizer President, Interstel Councilmember Sy. Blyreena Ekstafor

Rotation 2, Mayak Harvest, 3550

...To whoever is listening to this, or translating it word by word, or reading its transcript, know that this last piece of wisdom I have of his to share, this last gift...

It is for you.

Enter Auxiliary Speaker: Ovlan Faranawe

It's a little odd being told by your place of work: *Plan for certain death. Just in case.*

But I see the sense in it. I see the wisdom in a last stand well before any conceivable deathbed. Sometimes I wonder if everyone, even children, should make one as soon as we are able. There are so many of us who aren't able, or aren't given the opportunity, to reflect, to say some parting words before we go. It's a bit macabre, but I feel lucky to be spurred to do so, even if it makes me slightly suspicious of murder in the night.

Let's see. Let's think.

Our existence, whether you believe it is spiritually ordained or an outcome of evolution, is unified under the term *life*. Plants are alive. Bugs are alive. Snakes…ah, but how I wish it weren't so… snakes are alive. Life, movement, existence—this is what unites us with everything. With every species in the stars that we have not discovered, with our friends, our lovers, our bondmates, our families, our pets, and our enemies. We are all alive. It is the single greatest and most important unifying experience we all share.

You would think that alone would build empathy. That all of us having been blessed with, or serendipitously thrown into, a chance to experience a small fraction of all time in the universe would make us kinder to each other or the world kinder to us. But it doesn't, a lot of the time. A lot of the time, due to other people, or our own actions, or plain circumstance, bad things happen. Things that terrify us. Things we can't control.

It is getting harder and harder to breathe. I have to take slow, deliberate steps now, or I will overexert myself, will find myself gasping for all the air I expelled too hastily. Pumpkin is looking back at me. I don't know if he's figured out why he's gotten better and I've gotten worse, but there is an urgency in his eyes, an anxiousness. He sniffs the ground in a circle and stares back at me, meows. *Hurry up*, he's saying. *This way*.

I take the longest breath of my life, and it does nothing. I step forward anyway.

It can sound like a betrayal of all that is good and reasonable to say: embrace the bad as part of you, your life, and your world, especially when so many die—many unjustly—or are killed in war, or by misadventure, or are slain in bed by disease. It feels like bleak surrender to try to make peace with all the things that have and do and will go wrong in our lives. Maybe it is impossible to do so. At the very least, we can't deny that they are there. That they have been there through all of history; that they will be there for all the history that is yet to be made. These bad things, too, are a part of life, the dark matter trails we trace between shining lights in our skies.

My mouth is dry, but my water supply ruptured alongside the air. Every step feels like it's about to fall through a cloud. I trip. I clatter to the ground. It takes a moment, a few swallows of what oxygen I have left, but I prop myself up on the wall, pull myself to a stand on splintered tubing.

Pumpkin waits for me. I pay attention to his eyes, how perfect and green they are, how pink his nose is.

There's a fork in the path. He sniffs each of them, and decides.

This way, he meows. *Hang on.*

This is not to say that in the face of the terrible, we should not fight. There is much evil in the world that can and will be made better by people bold enough to stand against it. There are wrongs that can be righted, traumas that can be prevented, mistakes that can be acknowledged and repaired.

But there are things that do not falter, do not wither, in the face of so much goodness. There are diseases that cannot be cured. There are accidents. Malfunctions. Natural disasters. There are resources that dwindle or are scarce. There are crops meant to feed for a whole season that spoil.

There is death.

Pumpkin stops at a dead end, a cave-in from above, a pyramid of rubble stacked to the ceiling. He yowls at it, thwarted. I suck in the last bit of oxygen in the tenth percentile. It drops to nine percent, and the klaxon can't be overridden anymore. It's sending out wireless signals. It's letting everyone and anyone within twenty kilometers know that the person in this suit is dying, and the person in this suit is me.

"It's okay, buddy." I sit cross-legged on the ground. I rest my helmet in my hands, my elbows on my knees.

He rushes to me. He bops my helmet with his own, telling me to get up. When I don't, he scampers back toward the towering wreckage. He yells at it. He howls at it. He's louder than even the klaxon.

Death comes for us all. Even suns die. Galaxies die. One day, the universe will die.

I can't help but think that my favorite paintings bear both the sun and the storm, or that all great stories—both in fiction and in our very lives—are necessarily touched by joy and sadness in fighting measures. I can't help but remember that love, for our partners, our families, our friends, is an invitation for grief. That's why I'm recording this, isn't it? That in the chance of my death, it might help my loved ones grieve. It might help the world grieve.

I stand here in this beautiful edifice to our people I am privileged to help build and, without knowing whether it will survive eons or not, am so proud to witness it now. I do not know how long this place will survive, how long our civilization will live, or me, or my bondmate, or Panev, or all the other planets we've colonized throughout the cosmos. What I do know is that I have right now. Only this moment is certain. Only this moment is. That is just as true when we are sad as when we are happy. I have fears and doubts about the future, regrets about the past, surely. But realizing our finiteness, acknowledging where we are, is how we reconcile it. It's how we move forward. It's how we live our lives to the fullest, even when scared or in pain.

Death, like life, is the great unifier. We may not go all at once, but we all go together.

I hope that whoever is watching this, or reading it, or hearing it, that you do not suffer pain for too long if I go. I hope you one day recognize grief's beauty, learn to live with the shadows, to understand that the only reason they could be so dark is because they were cast by so much light.

Blyreena and Ovlan filled my cabin with light. She watched him with so much pride and, as he neared the end of his speech, stepped toward him. She rested her holographic head against his holographic shoulder. She smiled. When he finished, he smiled too. They stayed like that, a little while. And then they faded together.

The message in the cache had ended.

I grit my teeth, force myself to stand.

Oxygen is at five percent. The klaxon is maddening, but I'm starting to not be able to hear it. Everything is sort of blurry, sort of blue-tinted. My headlamp has died, so only Pumpkin's light is illuminating the cave-in. He's climbed up halfway and is pawing at loose rubble. He's roaring at the ceiling. He's not strong enough to burrow out of here on his own. If I don't do something, he'll die not long after me, alone, watching me rot.

I grab a length of exposed, twisted rebar and pull. It won't budge. But I pull, and pull, and the nearby metal whines a little, just in time for the tank to hit one percent. The hissing stops. There's nothing left to spill out.

Something in the pile above me shifts. Dirt rains over me. Pumpkin leaps to the ground, leaving me in darkness. I breathe out, and choke.

"Life is a gift, Scout," my mom told me. "Yours is just for you. Every moment. Every second. Run with it. Cherish it. Breathe it all in, Scout. That's how you say thank you."

She pulled me to her. Either I was very heavy, or she very weak.

"Don't waste it," she said. "Don't ever give it away. Don't ever settle for something that doesn't make you happy. Okay, my baby? Never stop fighting to make the best of it. Never stop fighting to make it better."

Mom.

Here in the raining rubble and the dirt and the dark, in a moment that feels like the flash of a lifetime, I'm sorry. Because I'd left her after—left her to die alone—and because maybe I didn't even understand her last words to me, for here I am, having chosen Pumpkin over myself.

But she wouldn't be mad, would she? I think, quietly, against the blaring anxiety of all my other thoughts, that more than anyone, she would understand.

Thank you, I think.

I love you.

I breathe in. It is a full, long breath.

There is a hole in the ceiling, an emergency port in my side connected to Kieran's suit. He and June and Pumpkin are staring down at me, mouths moving. I can't hear a thing, but right now, I am just happy to see them. I am so happy to be alive.

Lo, I can breathe.

29

I come to on my back, staring up at the inside of a dark, hollow metal dome. Its ceiling is at least two hundred meters high, barely lit by a smattering of emergency lanterns spread out over the floor. Verity Co. design, by the looks of them. The room is littered with administrative clutter, like on Panev.

A face looms into view directly over me. Kieran blinks, surprised. "Whoa! You're awake. Hey! They're awake!"

He calls toward the center of the room, where a slightly circular raised platform reminds me of the command center we saw—also on Panev. June's prim, clicking footfalls register before her shadowy figure does. Pumpkin darts in from somewhere and bops my helmet with his.

"Meow," he says.

"Hi, buddy." I reach to pet him but stop at the pain, wincing.

"Hey," Kieran says and helps put my arm back on the floor. "Go easy. You almost died."

"That's reassuring."

June arrives beside me. She takes a metal wand off her belt and presses it to the crook of my arm. There's a slight suction or magnetism where it touches, spreading the fibers of my suit so it can detect something through the thinnest amount of disturbance possible. The purple light on the wand's display glints off her helmet, and I catch a few fuzzy numbers and the image of a heart. My suit's computer must be badly damaged to have to take basic readings like heart rate manually.

She retracts the device with a neat little *click* and places it back on her belt. "Blood oxygen is back to normal. How's your head?"

"Throbbing like crazy," I say.

"That'll be a side effect of the cell stabilizer." At what must be my confused expression, she adds, "Something I gave you to help with the whole almost-braindead thing. Not breathing isn't so good for you, turns out."

"Thanks," I say flatly. "When can I expect the bill?" She frowns, and I feel a little bad. "Where are we, anyway?"

"The dome we were trying to get to," Kieran says.

"It was insane. June dragged me here through that deathtrap in the main path—"

"Perfectly navigable," she says.

"—and when we finally got in, we heard Pumpkin."

"And were receiving your SOS signal."

"We barely got to you in time." Kieran points to an area of the floor not so far away, where a hatch, cleared of rubble, stands open, the stone around its base cracked and sunken. "You were down there. There was so much in the way."

I manage to sit up carefully enough that the pain is minimal. Now that I can breathe, my other bodily problems are demanding attention. My back hurts, my arms hurt, my head hurts. Pumpkin walks into my lap and curls up to nap.

"What happened with the Remnant?" I ask. "How did we even survive it?"

"June," Kieran says, almost like he's disappointed. "Verity Co. has a grenade that can explode outside of the perimeter it's detonated in."

"Not quite," June interrupts. "More like, the initial explosion is harmless, but as it expands..." She extends her hands and wiggles her fingers, implying the harmful shock wave.

"A weapon that works against the Remnants," Kieran says, again disappointed.

"You can kill them?" I ask, half in awe, half in disgust. I think about all the Archivists whose lives could have been saved by not only being able to detect them but also destroy them.

"Of course not," she says. "Not even Verity Co. has found a way to kill them for good. The ERD"—she sighs—"the external repulsion detonator prevented your cellular death for exactly the two seconds I needed to knock you through the wall with a sonic rocket."

"That explains the bruised ribs."

"Please. It was half-broken already. You'd know if I forced you through anything solid."

"So the ERD is just, what? A heat wave?" Kieran asks.

June nods. "Superheated air deters the Remnants. Temporarily."

"So it's still out there."

"Absolutely. The force they exert is strong, but not so strong they can break through walls. If they did, we would have died back on Planet Designated 45-x9."

Galan, I think.

"So it's out there," she says, "probably back where we left it, looking for some trace of life to snuff out."

We all think about that for a moment. The dome is silent, save for Pumpkin's purring.

I shift a little with the discomfort of the question I'm about to ask. "So, would this ERD thing, would it not have saved Gunner?"

June sighs, short and agitated, like she knew the question was coming. "Of course it would have. And we'd used two just getting to where we had when we ran into you two. But he was taken too fast. I hardly had time after..." She stops and closes her eyes tight.

Kieran averts his eyes to study his hands. I give Pumpkin a massage. June isn't going to finish that thought.

"Thank you," I say slowly, for real this time. "No offense to Kieran, but without you, I'd be dead."

"It's true," Kieran says.

"Yeah, well." June throws her hands up, exasperated. "What's another protocol violation?"

She mutters that last part so softly I barely catch it. It's directed enough at herself that I don't prod, but I wonder: What *would* Verity Co. do to her if they caught her sharing these trade secrets? Have other Archivists run into other Verity grunts and learned these things? Would anyone believe me if I talked about it, if I accused their company of withholding life-saving technology?

As if that would be anything new.

I massage Pumpkin and look over the room. So many desks, so many chairs, but bedrolls too. Half-decayed metal bottles. Piles of eroded fabric—blankets, maybe clothes. This place was a holdout in the end. A refuge. There's not a single body to speak of, though.

The only trace of the last living Stelhari there could be is in a cache.

June follows my eyes to the command center. The weapons on her belt are within easy reach, and there's tension in her crossed arms.

"Have you taken it?" I ask.

"Not yet. Was busy saving you, remember? And setting a perimeter."

"If there's a readied message," I say, "please, please let us see it. This is their last cache, and..." And I have to know. I need to know what they found.

June bites her lip but nods. She's not looking me in the eye, but off to the side somewhere. "We'll watch it together," she says. "Turn it on."

After a little bit of work, Kieran and I do.

30

The cache emitter forms a hologram of Nyaltor, the same scientist we saw after accessing the cache on Nebul. He stands tall but beaten, his eyes slightly sunken, his interlaced fingers fidgeting. He's exhausted. "This is Panev's head of Sciences, Nyaltor Vekterran," he says.

"Contained in this database is the culmination of two decades of research into the phenomenon we call Endri. It is the very phenomenon that has consumed our capital world. It has consumed Nebul. A week ago, it consumed Galan. And as of this morning, we can no longer trace the signal of any colonized planet within our empire. We believe this research base to be the last bastion of our people.

"Though we are unsure of the mechanism that allows it to do this, Endri has spread rapidly and virulently through our worlds. The scale and immediacy of its destruction go beyond what we could have anticipated.

"We first theorized the existence of Endri twenty-one years ago, after the arrival of one of our probes to the Petr galaxy. It landed on an exoplanet covered with the ruins of an ancient civilization and evidence of another sentient, intelligent species. The planet was a colorless wasteland, and all mechanisms that could have once allowed for life were absent. The planet bore no water, no vegetation, no air. Not even trace microbes existed—not in the atmosphere, not in the ground. There was evidence of whole oceans having dried up, whole trenches cut deep into the planet's crust with not a trace of fossil or corpse. The planet was utterly devoid of life *and* the chemical forces necessary to reconstruct it. Worse, those forces could not be restarted. Terraforming efforts were, even after years, entirely ineffectual. We had never seen anything like it.

"All other planets explored in that cluster had faced the same fate. When we discovered Remnants, such as we had, we realized they were a small aspect left behind from the greater whole. Our first efforts were to capture them. With authorization from Interstel we sent in a specialized exoplanet military task force alongside a dozen alien, forensics, and ecological researchers. What they found was that the Remnants were nearly impossible to subdue.

"Sonic, force, and ballistic weaponry have little to no effect. Even antimatter and dark-matter weaponry, some of our most advanced, leaves no mark. Heat-emitting devices were most effective, including lasers and pinpoint nuclear strikes. But even these seemed only to quell Remnants or, at their most effective, cause the entities to vanish, then simply reappear later. Thousands of hours of combined combat data against the Remnants cost a third of the military personnel and half of the researchers their lives."

I look at June. Her face is set, her mouth a thin grim line.

"But in the end, exactly one Remnant was captured and stored successfully, then delivered at once to the specialized research base on Galan. Over years, the team there discovered there was no way to sample the essence of the Remnant. We considered that they might be made of dark matter, given their appearance, but it is as if the entity takes physical shape without *being* matter. The laws of nature seem not to apply to them at all. The deaths they cause are particularly suspect. Contact with the Remnants causes instantaneous death, or, more appropriately, vanishment. Contact leaves behind no evidence of the person or creature that was: no skeleton, no bioorganic matter, nothing at all.

"Most fearsome is that these Remnants are but paltry aspects of the entity that left them behind. While the Remnants are dangerous, they react aggressively toward life in only a relatively small vicinity and are dormant otherwise. It is hard to believe that even a hundred of these creatures could wipe out an entire planet in mere hours or minutes. They travel at speeds comparable to a Stelhari's average running speed and cannot penetrate through bulkheads, adequately powered force fields, or even walls. Whatever came before—whatever left them behind—cleaves through these things and more, as is evidenced by the slashed, jagged ruins of the planets where the Remnants are found.

"While the Remnants and their bearer have been scientific fascinations for our Exoplanet Research Division, we had no way to know that these things—that what had left them behind—could pose any threat to us. We thought them an alien species, a plague, a phenomenon for another world.

"Roughly one year ago, we received the highest-level alert from Ipsi, a planet in one of our edge systems. It is an alert reserved for global calamities: significant natural disasters, extinction-risk meteor strikes, pandemics, foreign invasions… Our emergency squadrons arrived in a week's time to a planet gone cold, lifeless, and gray.

"Ships in orbit around the planet and ones within

range of an emergency vessel launch were found empty. Planet-side investigators discovered the wreckage of a flourishing world that was. They discovered that nuclear payloads had been launched. They discovered that there were no bodies, no evidence of any life, no flora or fauna at all. They discovered Remnants.

"We have never encountered Endri in space. We do not know how it moves from place to place. We have not even encountered this entity, only its remains. When it is done with its grim work, it simply seems to vanish, to reappear or warp elsewhere.

"It is antilife, simply stated. Why it doesn't deteriorate all matter, such as the rock of planets' crusts or our structures, is completely unknown to us."

Pumpkin meows at my brother's feet, a small, sad chirp. Kieran picks him up and squeezes.

"Interstel responded quickly to the threat," Nyaltor goes on, "declaring a galactic emergency. We had no idea how little time we had to act. There were only weeks between whole planets going dark. Our ships could hardly move so fast and effectively through so much space.

"All divisions across all planets were ordered to dedicate their time to solving the Endri Crisis. The Sciences coordinated from every angle: biological, physical, metaphysical. We brought in the Builders and the military wings to coordinate on effective weaponry. Educators pushed bright, forward-thinking students to the front lines well ahead of their time. Financers imposed taxes, dove into emergency resources, fast-tracked mining operations for valuable fuel. Everyone was tasked with doing anything to aid in resolving this threat.

"There was one finding by the researchers at the Histories on Nebul. Hundreds of years ago, our ancient ancestors, just beginning to move from system to system, discovered a derelict vessel in space. On it was a single corpse belonging to an alien species utterly and entirely biologically distinct from our own, as well as its last stand: an electronic journal left behind in the ship's logs, which were dated an estimated two hundred years before the floating vessel was even discovered.

"The preserved corpse and its journal were entombed in the Histories Visitor Center, celebrated as our first contact with an alien species. Though its last stand had been combed through by the historians of our past, the Endri Crisis brought new light to the alien's entries. It had indicated a star-eating star, a darkness sweeping across planets. It had spoken of a weapon it had helped create, one it had been tasked with setting off, but didn't.

"At the time, and even decades after the derelict's discovery, researchers had considered these the final ramblings of a world too far removed from ours to be of any mortal concern. Fiction, or simply an intellectual fascination. The alien ship's trajectory had brought it on a course from a direction we were not able to map, a cluster of systems we were not—even with our technology—able to reach.

"Now, in light of this crisis, the alien's warning of 'sky-painted monstrosities swallowing worlds' strikes an inevitable chord, highlights an inevitable missed opportunity. On reflection, and with our understanding of the greater universe, we have been able to deduce several likely starting points for this dead ship's voyage. Perhaps it will be of help to whoever finds this.

"The alien's translated and original records have been stored in this cache thanks to the tireless efforts of Nebul's historians. Absolutely everything that we believe can be linked to the Endri, every historical finding, every artifact, every piece of scientific discovery, has also been catalogued here. All that we have been able to discover, deduce, theorize is in this sealed data collation. It should survive when destruction finds us." Nyaltor nods to someone the emitter doesn't show. He swallows.

"Endri is worse than death," he says. "Life has necessary endings: cycles and rebirths giving way to new starts. Endri is stagnation. It blankets our universe in a gray film in which no life can begin anew, enacting a cold, unmoving universe, the termination of the cycles that have allowed for countless eons of life. It is the most vital threat imaginable to all living things. We urge anyone who remains, anyone who finds this, please: take our findings. Use them. Find a way to rescue this universe from its true, final end."

31

Nyaltor vanishes and the emitter flickers off, returning the cavernous dome to the dim, ambient light of our headlamps and lanterns, the quiet of my own breathing and my own pulse.

"They gave up," June says. "I thought—how stupid—I thought maybe you were right, you know? Maybe they found something that could save us from this."

I look at her. "Were you even listening to him? They fought as long as they could with what they had. They pooled all the resources in their civilization to meet this threat."

"And then they didn't."

I don't know how to retort, not immediately. They didn't, she's right. The Stelhari did everything they could and still couldn't meet the Endri threat, and in the end they couldn't resist it. They are all dead. But—

"But they tried," I say.

"So?"

"They compiled everything they found, all their lives' worth of research and effort, the last hope of their civilization, for us."

When you love someone or something, sometimes it doesn't even matter what happens to you. You just want to see whatever it is you're rooting for succeed. Or *survive.*

June throws up her hands so fast and with such frustration that Pumpkin startles from the motion. "You heard him. Nothing can be done. Antimatter, dark matter, nuclear weaponry—nothing can stop it. It's not an enemy that can be beaten. If it comes for us, we're dead too."

"They mentioned another galaxy—a weapon, maybe."

She laughs. "Maybe," she says, drawing the word out long and cynically. "What's the point? What's the point in resisting against something impossible to overcome?"

There's a frantic edge to her voice, like she's fighting with me to understand her point of view. Like she knows with all the certainty of the cosmos that she's right on this one and is being driven insane by the fact I can't see it too. It's so intense, I think: *Maybe I am wrong. Maybe there is nothing to hope for, to work for, to dream for.*

But I think of Mom. I think of Blyreena and Ovlan.

"What's the alternative?" I say. Kieran looks at me, worried. It's his *don't poke the lady with the gun* look, but I keep going. "We turn our backs on everything they built for us? We don't try anything? We might all die, so let's give up now? Is that it? Is death a concession that nothing matters?"

"It's futile," June snaps. "You want to bury your head in the sand and pretend this isn't inevitable."

"No. I want to make the best of what the Stelhari have given to us."

"They couldn't even make the best of what was given to *them*. All these messages, they look miserable. They look like they knew the world was ending. The pain they must have been in. The pain Gunner..." She closes her eyes. "There's nothing here the Archivists could use to save us from the Endri."

"You can't just go all or nothing," Kieran starts, but June draws her weapon and he closes his mouth. Pumpkin hides behind him.

I laugh, disappointed but not surprised. "You're going to shoot us? After all this?"

"Only if you get in my way," she threatens.

Without any fanfare, I decide to get in her way. I feel my face flush. Outside, it might look like frustration, but that's not it. I'm not frustrated anymore. I'm not tired or confused or even angry. I'm focused. I'm determined. I march straight to the cache.

June traces me with her gun. "Scout. I will shoot you."

"Scout," Kieran says, wary. "June, hang on."

I lean next to the cylindrical casing and start going through files on its little screen. June's footsteps clack up behind me, and I see the metal edge of a gun reflecting off the inside of my cracked and battered helmet. The reflection catches the light of her own helmet, and she's faceless, just a wall of glass.

Pumpkin bounds to me and presses urgently into my calf, but I don't stop to console him. I don't hear the details of Kieran's pleading. I just see: *Weapon tests data. Defense systems—remote data. Defense systems—local data. Hello World. Remnant case one collation. Endric collapse manifesto—Panev.*

"June," Kieran says, closer now. "Listen—"

I find what I'm looking for.

There's a flash. A pop. The gun has turned in that reflection, not toward me, or my brother, or Pumpkin, but toward a new holographic figure who's appeared. A hundred new figures who've appeared.

The emitter atop the cache has sent out holograms all over the dome. June's fired at one of those. Kieran's got his hands over his head. Pumpkin's buried his head in my boot. Words are flowing out of the holographic crowd, the ones closest to us artificially louder over the din.

"—all we could," one says.

"—my dad, my uncle," another says.

"—the trees, the wind, but most of all, my love, I—"

June relaxes. My brother relaxes. Pumpkin lifts his head off my boot and goes to sniff at the nearest hologram. He looks up at them and meows, but they keep talking. *I wish I could have told you*, they're saying.

June looks at me. "What is this?"

"Their last stand," I say.

"—I was never brave enough to—"

"—remember when she rode it into Grandma's tiered cake? Spirits, he was mad."

"It's like, their last words," I go on. "The things they wanted to say, what life meant for them, what they wanted for their loved ones and friends. Their beliefs. What they hoped to give to the world before they went."

June, still clasping her weapon, cautiously wanders between the figures. I follow. She stops at a pair of Stelhari, studies them. The emitter projects the sounds of their voices toward us, dimming the conversations of the ones we've left behind.

"I'm so scared," one of them says.

"Just try," says the other. "Be here. This is all we have. This is what we have left."

"I can't. It's too much."

"Okay. That's okay, really. I'm here with you. Is that alright?"

The first figure sobs and nods. The two embrace. June turns away. I follow her to another hologram, passing Kieran. He's wandering too. Pumpkin paws at the figures, tries to get them to play with him. June studies each face we pass, almost like she's searching for something.

"—the sea where we met, in every dream I have, waking and otherwise. Down to the very detail, every grain of sand—"

"—can't wait to see you again—"

"—glad we had the opportunity to meet, to be—"

We stop beside a Stelhari outfitted in stark contrast to most. It's clear he's combat-able, strapped with exotic weaponry and belts, armored from head to toe in an exoskeleton that makes his already impressive height astounding. He has a long gun in his grip, a true soldier at attention, but like all the rest, he's speaking.

"—want you to know that I'm happy to do it," he says. "That this is the life I wanted, that I would have chosen it even if you didn't push me into it."

June goes stock-still.

"It wasn't always perfect, but..." The Stelhari chuckles, then frowns, slowly. "I hope you survived on Galan. They told me it's gone now, but you were always tougher than most, right? And now it's my turn. The Endri is here. I'll fight it with everything I have, the way I know you did. Maybe we'll run into each other in the void, huh?"

He raises his gun. He points it to where the floor is sunken now, toward the maintenance shaft my brother and June pulled me out of. All the holograms turn in that direction. Their eyes widen. Their mouths open. The sound cuts before we hear them scream. The emitter flickers, and every one of them vanishes.

We're left again in the relative dark, just the four of us.

June paces. I watch her. Kieran and Pumpkin walk up beside me.

June finally stops to glare at me. "Why?" She says this like I've hurt her.

"The Stelhari I've gotten to know through the cache copy we made on Panev believed in every moment," I say slowly. "And I think these ones did too. Because, June, all those moments are worth fighting for, even if things that are gone won't come back…even if we all die, in the end." I take a deep breath. "We can make the best of right now. We can serve these people's memories—the memories of everyone who has lost their life to the Endri and its Remnants. And they wanted us to carry on. Trust me. Even if they died, they wanted us to live. The Stelhari. Gunner." I look at Kieran. "Mom. We can carry them with us into a better tomorrow. We can fight for a better tomorrow, even if we don't believe it will come. That's all we can do. For ourselves. And for them."

June shakes her head. Laughs, huffy and despondent. She paces a small, helpless circle. She looks around the room. At the cache. At Kieran. At Pumpkin. At me. At where the armored Stelhari stood.

"Shit," she says. "Take it."

"You're not going to shoot us in the back, right?" Kieran—always on the lookout.

She looks around the room again and puts her pistol to her belt at last. "No," she says sadly. "You three would just haunt me, I think."

32

Kieran is able to temporarily reactivate the command center, which allows June to lower the dome shielding. It grinds and folds almost perfectly back into place within those slots in the floor, and while we expect the Remnant below to stir at the noise, June assures us that it doesn't.

Her dinghy is parked outside the main dome, not too far from ours. She remotely cancels its cloaking device, and we all stand in the wide space between our ships, thinking through how to say goodbye.

June crosses her arms. "So," she says.

I nod. "So."

"What, now that I've given you a cache, you finally don't have something to say?" I know she's teasing by the slight crook of her mouth, even if her voice is just as stern as usual.

"Thank you," I say. "It means more than you know that you're letting us take this." I wave back at Kieran, who's got the cache strapped to him. He smiles in agreement.

"Some of the information on there might be on the caches we still have, you know."

"What would that mean?"

She shrugs, tired and a little uncaring. "I don't know. Usually when Verity Co. scours a system, they get the whole payload."

"*They*, huh? Not *we*?" I smile, but she just shrugs again.

"Are you going to be okay?" Kieran asks.

"Probably," she says, and then, with less conviction, "Maybe. I'll argue that without Gunner, you two just got the better of me down here."

"Will that work?" I ask.

"I don't know. I have no idea what happens when we get home. Hopefully, they'll be placated by the fact I'm bringing them anything at all."

Kieran looks at me, worried.

"But that's not your concern, is it?" June says. "You have what you wanted, and we'll probably never see each other again."

That hurts, and I'm surprised. I'm not crazy about her. We're not friends or anything close, but, well.

When it's just you, your brother, your cat, and a mercenary lady out in the dark of space, you can't help but cling to what little life around you there is. I think I hide the sentiment well enough.

"I guess you're right," I tell her. I approach, grasp her under the elbow as she does the same to me. "Thank you, June."

"Don't die out there, Scout."

We let go. She says goodbye to Kieran and—to my continued surprise—gives Pumpkin an enthusiastic scratch.

"And seriously," she calls, walking backward to her dinghy. "Space is no place for a cat!"

We wave goodbye, board our own way home. June takes off first, and I follow the sleek black vessel with my eyes until it disappears against the stars.

Back aboard the *Waning Crescent*, Kieran and I celebrate with a pizza. Actually, two pizzas. We've set our course for home and are playing *Smash 'Em Dead*, blasting too-happy music, and knocking back beers without any fear for the next day's hangover.

We're hungover, and we should have been afraid.

There's these little pills you can take for that. They're packed with electrolytes and other stuff, I don't know. "Just give me the damn pill," I say, interrupting Kieran's reading of the package. My head feels like a nuclear reactor mid-meltdown.

"Damn. Yikes. Fine." He hands me the pill. "You're just mad that I beat you with Kahoot."

"Because he's cheap as shit. You're cheap as shit."

"Cheap as shit but with a better killstreak than you!"

I throw my ration at him. He dodges it like a stupid bunny-hat-wearing pink ninja and squeaks, "*Kahoot!*"

We're eating Archivist-standard food for dinner. We've got a few pizzas left and a long journey home, so we're saving them. Pumpkin is eating beside us, a rare occasion. Kieran baited him with an even rarer can of tuna. We all eat in comfortable silence, the blurred lines of jump space gliding out the window.

In the morning, I leave my cabin and follow the peppy, poppy music to the cockpit. I worked all night, categorizing the data sets from the new cache, so I'm grateful to see a carafe of the good stuff there, even if it is a spill risk for the dashboard. Kieran knowingly pours me a space-safe mug and hands it to me as I take my seat in the copilot's chair.

We're quiet for a little while, then we talk for a little while, about nothing, really. Then we're quiet again. Pumpkin appears out of nowhere, as cats are wont to do, and hops into my lap. He burrows deep and falls fast asleep.

"Kieran," I say.

He looks at me casually, but seeing my face, turns serious. "What's up?"

"I'm sorry I got mad at you when you told me you wanted to stay home after all this. It wasn't fair."

"Oh." He releases some visible tension, sits back in his chair. "Thank you."

"I just didn't want to lose you. And so soon after Mom"—I sigh—"after Mom died. It felt like losing another family member when you told me. But," I say, before he can interrupt, "I know that's not what it is. I know you just have a different direction you want to go in, and that's okay. I'm okay. I support it. And you."

Pumpkin rolls onto his back and purrs. I give him pets.

"Thank you," my brother says again. "I wish I could say I've changed my mind, but it's really what I want to do."

I nod. I've always known he doesn't enjoy this life as much as Mom and I, but I hoped maybe he'd come to love it over time, that our first outing with just the two of us would finally help him see everything that *I* love about being out here. "I know. It's, uh, it's hard to imagine being out here without you. No one has my back quite the same."

"You'll be okay. And you won't be alone." He smiles. "Headquarters barely approved just two of us being out here, remember? You'll probably have a whole team of people."

"Yeah," I say quietly. It's not a comforting thought now, but I trust that one day it will be.

"And you'll always have a place to come back to," he says. "I might even relocate us near our favorite pizza place."

I laugh. "Or you can finally start your own shop."

"Nah. I think the Archivists will have plenty of work for an engineer home-side."

"Probably. Just, no Verity Co."

"I solemnly swear."

Pumpkin rolls back over, drooping like a giant, heavy blanket over my legs. I pet him relentlessly, letting his warm fur and happy trills bring some comfort to all this sadness. I watch the stars blurring past the cockpit window, the swirling, rainbow path home. I tell myself, *Everything will be okay.*

"Hey," Kieran says. "Movie sounds kind of fun, doesn't it?"

I wipe my eyes. "Yeah, it does."

"So… *Robot Invasion 3* or… *Robotsylvania*?"

"Duh," I laugh. "It's a classic."

"I'll go make some popcorn."

"Meet you there," I say.

I don't know what the future will bring, whether the new team I'll have at my back will be able to replace the companionship I feel with my brother, whether Pumpkin will go with me or him, whether anything that we've found in this cluster will actually help save us from the Endri, or whether that entity will even come for us at all. It's scary, looking ahead. It's sad, looking back, remembering the time I had with my mom, the times I *could* have had with her; remembering that there was a time I was sure Kieran and I would be out here among the stars for life; remembering that once upon a time, in the stars behind us, there was someone named Blyreena and someone named Ovlan who loved each other very much.

I don't know what the future will bring, but I know that right now, Pumpkin is with me, my brother is with me, and that we're about to go watch an amazing, terrible, impossible movie with robot vampires. I get up with Pumpkin, who trots eagerly beside me toward the den, and I tell myself, *This one is.*

★★★★★

ACKNOWLEDGMENTS

In the self-published edition of this work the acknowledgments were about half a page long. I began with: *Though writing can be a lonely voyage, few books are ever a solo endeavor.* This was true for me then, even with my (very) small publishing team of encouraging friends and family, and it is ever more true now. Sharing Scout's adventure with the world opened up my own personal world more than I ever imagined possible. I've met fellow authors, wonderful readers, kind booktubers and bloggers, publishing professionals, and friends who have all helped tremendously in bringing this book to you in its shiny new edition.

To start, this version of *The Last Gifts of the Universe* would simply not exist without my editor Kate

McHale, whose first email to me about the book will forever be a cherished memory. Kate brought deft, careful attention to the book's minor revisions to help polish it to a shine while remaining excited and supportive of the original version. What we came to is absolutely the definitive, polished edition of this story. I'm so grateful for Kate's enthusiasm, encouragement, and care in helping the book through the entire publishing process.

Thank you also to Rose Waddilove, Gemma Wain, and the entire proofreading team for those small changes that nonetheless created huge improvements, and to all of Del Rey UK for your kindness, patience, and support along the way. Especially enormous thanks to Ing Lee, a great artist and a great person both, who designed the incredible cover for this book and made Pumpkin unbelievably cute (for which, really, we all must thank her). Thanks also to Peter Joseph, Eden Railsback, and the kind folks over at Hanover Square Press for their support and work on the North American version of *Last Gifts*.

All the thanks in the universe to my agent, Valentina Sainato, who has been with me for every step of this publishing journey, and without whom I would surely have lost some sanity. Your breadth of knowledge about the industry and patience in helping me through it are more appreciated than you know. Thanks also to the entire team at JABberwocky; the cheers of support mean the world.

Before my journey into traditional publishing began, there were a number of people in the industry who read the self-published edition of *Last Gifts*, chatted with me, supported me, and encouraged me to keep writing. These people offered their knowledge and guidance freely and kindly, making it possible to take the book to where it is now. Thank you to Laura Bennett, Sunyi Dean, and Michael Mammay for all the help, with an extra nod here to Mike for introducing me to Valentina, for which I'm wordlessly grateful.

I would be remiss to not acknowledge the SFF indie and self-publishing community for their friendliness, generosity, and role in elevating my work. It is a community absolutely brimming with talented authors, kind readers, and passionate book content creators, and I am so lucky to have found supporters and friends among them. There are far too many people who have made this journey bright to name them all, but I especially want to thank A. R. Witham and the Keymark Community, G. M. Nair, S. Kaeth, Justin Gross, Craig (of the *Bookwyrm* variety), Kriti and *Armed With a Book*, Amanda and *Bookish Brews*, and of course Isabelle of *Shaggy Shepherd Book Reviews*, Pumpkin's first and most enthusiastic fan.

Thank you to the Self-Published Science Fiction

Competition (SPSFC), its hosts Hugh Howey and Duncan Swan, its master organizer, Scott, and especially to the many volunteer judges who selflessly give their time to reading and reviewing the hundreds of books which have been in the competition each year. I feel extremely honored that *Last Gifts* took first place in SPSFC2, and remain endlessly grateful for how many people cheered it through to the end.

Something I never thought I would have to do was take a professional author photo. Especially because of the time and effort that went into coordinating it, I want to shout out Rafael Rodrigues, the photographer, Charlotte, the world's best, most talented hair stylist, and Heather Cole, Curator and Specialist Librarian at the John Hay Library, where I was honored to do the shoot. You all made that day so much more fun than I was prepared for.

Of course, I could not have done any of this without my original team, those close few friends who read the earliest drafts of this book and encouraged me to share it with the world. Thank you to Liz, Greg, Maya, and Tammy Salyer, the self-published edition's original editor, whose suggestions and tweaks still survive today to help make this book shine. And to Conrad, for your love, partnership, and all those late-night chats helping me unravel plot holes. You're the light of my life.

Lastly, thank *you*, dear reader. In a world full of entertainment options, I am so grateful to you for choosing to spend your time with this book. I hope you got something back in return.